P.S. He's Mine!

Rosie Rushton & Nina Schindler

Piccadilly Press • London

First published in Great Britain in 2000
by Piccadilly Press Ltd.,
5 Castle Road, London NW1 8PR

Text copyright © Rosie Rushton & Nina Schindler, 2000

A catalogue record for this book is available from
the British Library

ISBNs: 1 85340 539 6 (trade paperback)
1 85340 544 2 (hardback)

1 3 5 7 9 10 8 6 4 2

Printed and bound by WBC, Bridgend

Design by Judith Robertson
Set in 10pt Courier and 10.5pt Gill Sans

@@@

To: Friederike Hofmann <ahofmann@uni-bremen.de>
From: Ellie Finch <elliefin@email.com>
Date: Wed, 30 Aug 2000 21:40:32
Subject: **How dare you!**

Dear Frederi . . . Frieder . . . Dear Freddie,
Surprised to hear from me? I bet! I guess you
thought you could get away with your devious
little tricks undetected. Dream on! I got my camp
newsletter today, with everyone's phone numbers
and e-mail addresses - which means I can zap this
to you right now and tell you just what I think
of you! Not that I think of you more often than
I have to - I don't want to pollute my mind.

I suppose you think you've been really clever
- not that there's anything new in that; you
spent the whole four weeks at Lac Léon acting
as though you were a cut above everyone else at
camp. Well, you're not - and for your
information, Marc reckons you're a dweeb too!

Oh yes - he told me that you sent him an
e-mail the very second you got home; it arrived
as he was halfway through the mega-long e-mail

he was writing to me, if you must know! He
told me all about it – because some people are
honest in their relationships, which is
something your devious little mind would find
hard to understand, I guess.

Ellie Finch turned from the keyboard and grabbed the e-mail
she had printed off moments before. Her eyes scanned the
two paragraphs and she bit her lip. Marc – gorgeous,
wonderful, sexy Marc – hadn't said that much about Friederike
actually – but then again, with just a little doctoring . . .
  She turned back to the screen.

He says that he had a very twee note from
little Rieke Hofmann which he supposed he would
have to reply to as it was all part of the job
of camp counsellor to be friendly to everyone
and besides, he had to forward you the camp
newsletter. So when you get his e-mail, DON'T
start imagining that you two are an item because
you're not. And never will be.
  You may have stolen the part of Portia from
me in the camp play, you may have bagged the
best seat on the coach on every single trip
out and you may, because of your oh-so-loaded
mummy and daddy, have sucked up to everyone by
buying them chocolate and cake every day, but
you needn't think you can swan in and take
Marc off me.

4

Remember, it was me he danced with at the
end-of-camp disco, not you. Anyway, didn't you
say you liked your precious horse more than
people? So go ride it.
With love (No way, cross that out!)
Goodbye!
Ellie

PS He's mine, and don't you forget it!

@@@

To: Ellie Finch <elliefin@email.com>
From: Friederike Hofmann <ahofmann@uni-bremen.de>
Date: Thu, 31 Aug 2000 18:30:14
Subject: **Leave me alone!**

SO WHAT? Go and tell your lies wherever you
want but leave me alone! You expect me to
believe that Marc wrote a long e-mail to you?
You know as well as I do that Marc's English
would not be good enough to correspond with you.
You think he's had a crash course since the
camp has ended? And don't tell me he wrote to
you in French because you certainly wouldn't
have a clue what "dweeb" would be in French!

The only thing you have in common with him is a big ignorance of foreign languages and don't expect me to excuse myself if I speak more than one language, because I did not like living in the USA for those two years and, rest assured, after this summer I don't like the English one tiny little bit better than the Americans!

No, Marc's letter to the one and only you was an official camp letter, composed by whomsoever to send to everyone, but I'm not astonished you've fallen for it the same way you fell for every guy who even deigned to smile at you! Who has got a devious little mind, then, by writing e-mails like this? As to my oh-so-loaded mummy and daddy: this really is nothing to lose YOUR sleep about, got that? What do you know about my family life? Nothing. At least I was not all the time at camp moaning and tossing and turning about a letter from home like some other people I could mention here! Toss and turn and moan as long as you want to, but don't pester me again with stupid lies — OK?
F.

PS You call that dancing? I would prefer another expression — perhaps clinging? Or engulfing? Or devouring? Sorry, my English vocabulary isn't up to your sort of behaviour . . .

Friederike took a long breath, swallowed deeply and pressed Send. Off you go! she thought jubilantly. And all my wrath, my fury, my humiliation!

How did she dare? That little beast! Poisoning what had been the most marvellous thing that ever had happened to Rieke! She closed her eyes and imagined herself back in the south of France, back in those woods of huge pine trees with their enticing smell, the flickering air at noon, when everything seemed to sizzle in the heat, the sun boiling down – and there she was again on that little path to the lakeside, and the shed in the woods, because there was someone waiting for her and the excitement and the breathlessness . . .

"FRIEDERIKE!" The voice of her mother.

Rieke started, opened her eyes and looked at the screen in front of her. "Coming!" she shouted and switched off her computer.

@ @ @

To: Friederike Hofmann <ahofmann@uni-bremen.de>
From: Ellie Finch <elliefin@email.com>
Date: Fri, 1 Sept 2000 09:01:57
Subject: **Grow up!**

You just can't bear to believe that when two people are in love, they will go to any lengths

to communicate with one another, can you? Marc's
English may not be as good as the oh-so-brilliant
Friederike I-Love-Myself-To-Pieces Hofmann's but
there are such things as dictionaries, you know!
Besides, words of love are universal . . .

Ellie surveyed that last sentence with a degree of pride. It had
a very nice ring about it. *Ich liebe dich. Je t'aime.* You didn't have
to be a star linguist to gaze into someone's eyes and know –
just positively, absolutely KNOW – that they loved you. What
was it Marc had called her? *Jolie, charmante.* Right, Miss
Hofmann, get a load of this . . .

. . . not that I'd expect you to understand,
considering no one has probably ever whispered
anything even mildly seductive into your ear.
And as for you accusing me of knowing nothing
about your family, that's rich! All we ever
heard about was how wonderful your brothers were
and how Basti was going bike riding (big deal!)
and how Mummy was some university high-flyer and
dearest Daddy travels the world being mega
clever with computers. Oh yawn, yawn! I notice
that none of them took time out to write to
you, though – unless you count that postcard
with three words scrawled on the back. And I
did not MOAN over my letters . . .

Ellie paused, searching her mind for some believable excuse for

8

the dreadful nightmare that her mother's news had induced. It shouldn't be difficult – after all, she'd been making up stories to hide the truth ever since she could remember. The trouble was, she didn't know exactly what it was she had said during those dreams – well, they were dreams really, weren't they? OK, so she was half awake, reliving that awful time when . . . No. Stop it. Come on. Get writing.

I guess if you had heard that your gran had fallen down in the road and narrowly missed being hit by a car, you might get a bit upset. **(That would do – after all, old people were toppling over all the time.)** Although, come to think of it, probably not. You're too wrapped up in yourself to care about anyone else. Let's face it, you did everything you could to get out of camp chores (did you ever wash up, one single time?) and you even refused to help backstage because you were the superstar.

And talking of bedtime, at least I grew out of taking soft toys to sleep with me when I was about seven, never mind stroking them and sucking my thumb! Hardly the sort of alluring behaviour that suggests you are anywhere near ready for a mature adult relationship with a man, is it?

A sudden, violent hammering on the front door shattered Ellie's thoughts. Her senses went on red alert. Was it . . . ? No. Please God, no. Not yet. Not again. Please.

She held her breath. She heard her mother's footsteps tapping along the tiled floor of the hallway. She swallowed, her throat tightening as it always did.

"Parcel – sign here, please!" the voice rang through the small terraced house.

Ellie let out her breath in one long gasp of relief. The postman. Thank you, God.

"Ellie!" Her mother's voice echoed up the stairs.

"Coming!" Ellie grabbed the mouse and scanned her eyes over what she had written. It was a bit – well, over the top. Maybe she should scrub out that bit about the soft toy and . . .

"ELINOR!" Her mother's voice suggested that delaying any longer would most definitely not be a good idea.

```
Now if you don't mind, I have a life to get on
with. May I suggest you go out and get one too?
Ellie

PS He's mine and don't you forget it!
```

She clicked on Send and zapped her message to Bremen. And good riddance.

@ @ @

Rieke sat motionless in front of her computer. She had only wanted to see if there was a new e-mail from Marc, as it had now been two long days without even a tiny little word from him – and there she was again! Ellie Finch, that unbelievably rude girl, that pest, who had tried so hard all those weeks to ruin her holiday . . . by trying to spoil the fun of putting on a real Shakespeare play . . . by telling dirty jokes and laughing her head off, when listeners like Rieke were shocked – well, not really shocked but certainly not amused – or had she behaved just like old Queen Victoria?

Rieke frowned. Why could that girl across the Channel annoy her so much? Why should she let her get again under her skin? She took a long breath and without even thinking her fingers started to touch the keys in front of her.

```
To: Ellie Finch <elliefin@email.com>
From: Friederike Hofmann <ahofmann@uni-bremen.de>
Date: Fri, 1 Sept 2000 09:53:06
Subject: Off you go!


Dear Miss Finch!
Would you please be so kind and erase my name
and address from your e-mail list? Let me remind
you that it was you who started throwing that
Internet garbage at me and as I'm not at all
interested in receiving more of that spiteful
dirt, I ask you very politely to leave me
alone.
  Go and write to whoever wants to be written
to by you – which I certainly don't. As to who
belongs to whom this is certainly not for you
```

alone to decide. May I therefore suggest you
leave that to the people concerned?

 There is really not all that much to be
thankful to you for, but if you could direct
your writing attentions to someone else I would
be awfully obliged.

FH

Rieke clicked on Send and let out a long breath. Only then she
realised that she'd typed the message with the speed of a
maniac. Damn! Why did she let that girl bother her so much?
There was nothing between that Ellie Finch and Marc!
Certainly not! Could not be! Those were all lies, made up to
hurt her! A poor revenge for being outdone at the play! And
all those snide remarks about her family? Why did Ellie envy
her so much? What was so funny about parents who were
almost never together at the same time, at the same place?
What was so mega-interesting about the money they earned
and which they obviously did not invest in that old barn they
called their house?

Had she really boasted as much as Ellie claimed? Hadn't it
been Anna, her best friend, who had always talked about
home and family? Well, Anna certainly had something to boast
about . . .

Rieke turned round, leaned over to her bed and grabbed
Fritz, her little black soft toy cat. "What stupid insinuations!"
she said to him angrily. "As if there never has been a boy who
was interested in getting your place in my bed! Come on,
Fritz, I love you still, because it was my big brother Anton who

12

gave you to me as a present when I was born. Well, he was already thirteen then, and it was kind of him to take notice of a baby sister!"

Rieke sighed. Yeah, it was nice to have big brothers – only they were off: three lived away from home and even Basti, who was only three years older, spent more time hanging around with his pals in Bremen than at home in a little village far away from "the scene".

Rieke felt lonely.

Time to get up and saddle Merlin and go for a long ride. Still alone, but with her horse – well, it was not so bad.

Before she got up Rieke switched off the computer. For some seconds she stood staring at the empty screen. No mail from Marc.

Well then. Maybe tomorrow. Something to look forward to. But if there was still nothing?

Should she write?

She squared her shoulders and threw Fritz back on the bed. No, she would not – repeat NOT – run after him.

But already, as she closed the door of her room behind her, she started to compose a letter to him . . .

Marc, mon chéri, je suis désespérée d'entendre de toi. Je ne sais pas comment survivre jusqu'à demain . . .

She sighed. No, right at that moment she really didn't know how she'd survive until tomorrow without hearing from him.

Yes, yes, YES!!! Ellie punched the air in triumph and galloped up the stairs two at a time. Now she had one over Freddie Hofmann – she couldn't wait to switch on the computer and get writing. She wished she hadn't sent that e-mail an hour before; what she had to tell Madam now would certainly wipe the smug smile off her precious little face.

She slammed her bedroom door, pushed the Power button and tapped her fingers impatiently while she waited for the screen to spring into life. Ping! New Message!

Surely not Freddie again? But then, who else was it likely to be? Marc! Of course – oh joy!

She clicked on the Inbox and scanned the screen.

Dear Miss Finch! Would you please be so kind ...

What on earth . . . ? Disappointment hit the pit of Ellie's stomach like a stone. Not Marc at all. Freddie.

. . . erase my name and address . . . not at all interested in receiving more . . .

Oh really? Well, she wasn't going to let her get away with that! Not with what she had to tell her.

To: Friederike Hofmann <ahofmann@uni-bremen.de>
From: Ellie Finch <elliefin@email.com>
Date: Fri, 1 Sept 2000 10:17:43
Subject: **You wish!**

Liebe Fraulein Hofmann (since you insist on such formality),

I was in the middle of opening Marc's parcel when your e-mail arrived. **(Brilliant – that should get her going!)** Bless him, he really shouldn't have – but I guess sending me something made him feel closer to me.

Well, she told her conscience firmly as a little knot of guilt settled itself in her chest, it's not a lie. He did send me something. OK, so it was only her blue cropped vest top that she'd left in the changing-rooms but the thing was, he knew it was hers. It didn't have a name tape sewn inside – the only way he could have known was if he'd taken such special notice of her each day that he'd seen her wearing it, and found the sight unforgettable. A little smile played on her lips as she imagined him standing under the shade of the great pine trees, secretly watching her diving off the springboard, or deliberately forgetting where he'd put one of the props for *The Merchant Of Venice*, just so that he could ask Ellie to bring it to him. Of course, if it hadn't been for Freddie, she, Ellie Finch, would have been playing Portia to Marc's Bassanio – but of course, Madam had muscled in, saying that she had already played the part at her American school and knew all the words.

Of course, I will now follow your suggestion and go and write to who I want to – Marc, actually, to thank him for the parcel and the lovely little note . . .

OK, so the note had been written on a scrap of paper and read *Hi Ellie, One day it will be your head that you are forgetting. Take care, Marc,* which as love-letters went was hardly an award-winner, but still . . . he had said "Take care", which must mean she mattered to him. He probably had someone standing at his elbow all the time he was writing and couldn't express his true feelings properly.

So why hadn't he e-mailed her again? What if Freddie was right, and that first e-mail was just a circular message he sent to everyone who had been at camp? But no – it couldn't have been. He'd actually said that he hoped she was feeling happier, and told her to remember all the things he'd said. As if she could forget – every word was etched on her memory for eternity.

. . . the French are so romantic, aren't they? Oh sorry - of course, you wouldn't know about that. I guess someone whose entire conversation revolves round some stupid horse can't expect mature men to engage in anything other than the most superficial of conversations.

She reread that last sentence and nodded in approval. She was good with words; Mrs Wilson at school was always telling her that. Ellie guessed it came from reading anything and everything in sight – it had certainly paid off with Marc.

She leaned back in her chair and thought back to that evening when he had found her crying by the old boatshed. Of course, she had been mega-embarrassed, especially since she knew that when she cried her nose went purple and her eyelids puffed up like a jellyfish. But he hadn't seemed to notice. He had simply flopped down on the grass beside her and silently offered her a handkerchief.

"You have sadness?" he had asked gently and Ellie had thought how much more poetic that phrase sounded than the usual impatient "What's the matter now?" she got from her mates at school on the days when the full horror of it all washed over her and she couldn't play-act any longer.

"You are missing your family, yes?" he had volunteered when she hadn't replied. As if!

"No way!" she had replied hastily, desperately racking her brains to think of an acceptable reason for her tears. "No – the thing is, I have . . ."

But just then the bell had rung for the first music workshop and Marc had jumped to his feet. "Come!" he had said, his tanned face crinkling in a smile. "We play – you feel better. Music, it is . . . how do you say . . . ?"

He frowned, clearly struggling for the right word in English.

"The food of love?" suggested Ellie, wiping her eyes and trying very hard to look laid-back and sophisticated.

Marc had flashed her a brilliant smile and clapped his hands. "So you are a Shakespeare lover, yes? Me also. So this is good – already we have something in common. So, come!"

And he had bent down, grabbed one of her hands and pulled her to her feet. She hadn't been able to speak. At the touch of his fingers little sparks of electricity shot up her arm, and her legs appeared to have turned to jelly.

"Perhaps," he said, heading off up the cinder path towards

the studio, "you will take part in the drama production, yes?"

Ellie had hesitated, thinking that her friend Lisa would be somewhat miffed if she backed out of the music and mime sessions. And she had intended to brush up on her singing. "Well . . ." she had begun.

"Me, I am to be producer," Marc had said proudly. "And I shall take a big part also. But of course, if you do not wish . . ."

"I wish," Ellie had said at once. "I wish very much."

And she would have had a part – a big part, she knew she would, if it hadn't been for that devious, scheming, self-opinionated . . .

I suppose you think (she began typing, her fingers speeding up as her temper increased,) that Marc gave you the part of Portia because he liked you. Well, let me put you in the picture. He chose you so that people wouldn't suspect about him and me.

Her fingers hovered for a moment. That was it! It must have been! Her subconscious mind had come up with the real truth.

And he put me in charge of props because . . . (She chewed her lip.) it meant we could spend time together working through the script and no one would guess what was really going on. Got it? Good! And now I will do what you asked and obliterate your name from my address list for

18

ever. Goodbye and good riddance. Have fun with
your horse! It has my sympathy.
Ellie Finch

Ellie scanned her eyes over what she had written. It was good, especially those last two paragraphs. And of course, that was how it had been. She just hadn't thought about it that way before. But it was obvious, wasn't it?

By the time she had switched off her computer and headed downstairs to the kitchen, she believed every word of the lie she had invented. But then she was good at lying. After all, she had been doing it for the past four years.

@ @ @

Friederike Hofmann slid from the saddle. Merlin had not been his usual bouncing self – he seemed slow and disinterested and the short gallop up the hill which he usually enjoyed so much had left him completely drained of all energy. She led him by the reins to the stable and took off the saddle. No, his coat was not smooth and silky, and his muscles didn't ripple – her beloved gelding was sick. She moaned inwardly. This meant the vet again, and the vet meant money . . . And since her return from France the Hofmann household had definitely been short of money. Even new clothes for the start of the school year had proved a problem.

"No, darling," her mother had said without even lifting her head from the student's paper she was correcting. "I don't have quite enough to see us through September, so take something from your savings if it is that important to you. Maybe I can give it back to you later in the year."

"But why?"

"And would you please shut the door behind you as I have rather a lot of work to do."

Rieke had left the room in a somewhat confused state of mind. What had happened? They had never been actually rich, but they had always been comfortably off – something that Ellie Finch must have guessed and envied her for. Well, she would ask Basti when he came home. But Basti spent most nights now in Bremen with his mates – they always had a sleeping bag for him when he wanted to stay.

Now she was afraid of having to tell her mother that Merlin needed the vet. But a close look at him confirmed her apprehensions. He was so changed. She carefully groomed his lacklustre coat, saw to the hay and the water and left the stable. She jumped on her bike and was home in five minutes.

Back home, she changed from her riding clothes to jeans and a sweatshirt and sat down at her desk. Goodness, that essay! What was it about?

She switched on the computer and while it sprang slowly to life she looked in her schoolbag for her copy book. Ah, there! "A Person Who Impressed Me" was the subject of the essay.

Well, who was a person who had impressed her? Her father? Up to last spring, perhaps. But during the last few months she had rarely seen him – either he was travelling for his computer firm or hidden in his room downstairs, working on new programmes or whatever.

She sighed. No, her beloved Paps was no longer a person who impressed her. Her eldest brother, Anton? Rieke shuddered when she remembered his latest girlfriend. Anton was not a bad guy, actually, but this Nicole . . . Hmm. No impression there either.

But . . . Rieke smiled, stooped down again and picked up the envelope she had hidden in the cover of her Maths book.

This was someone who'd impressed her all right: Marc. Though he was certainly no one she could write about in an essay for German composition. But soooo impressive . . . She took the letter out of the envelope and started reading the words she now knew by heart.

Ma chérie,
Il fait seulement trois jours que tu es partie et déjà je suis dévoré de désir de toi . . .

Rieke closed her eyes and tried to remember his voice. "*It is only three days since you left and already I am consumed by longing for you . . .*" She conjured up the many other times he whispered all kinds of sweet nonsense while caressing her neck with his lips. For a moment she thought she could feel his touch and smell his skin . . . but when she opened her eyes she was still sitting at her desk and the screen was waiting to be filled with words.

Without thinking, she went on-line and checked for mail.

Oh no. Ellie Finch again. But why? Hadn't she told her once and for all that she should leave her alone, with her snide remarks and her petty insinuations and that ridiculous assumption that Marc had cared for Ellie, just because he danced with her on the last evening . . .

As if he would have done that except for that terrible quarrel the afternoon before! But there had still been time for making up in the early morning hours, when they both had sat on the edge of Lac Léon, when the air coming in from the sea only ten kilometres away had been salty and fresh. And when the sun finally had come up on that very last day, Rieke had had to slip back into her bungalow, hoping none of the girls had realised that she had been gone all night. Ellie had been sleeping then, she couldn't have known that Rieke had silently sneaked out to meet her . . . what? Friend? Boyfriend? Lover?

No, nobody knew, not even Anna, who knew a lot but not everything.

Well, Miss Finch, Rieke thought, let's see where you'll try to put your poison this time! Rieke read the message quickly and before she knew it she was typing as fast as her fingers could find the right English letters.

```
To: Ellie Finch <elliefin@email.com>
From: Friederike Hofmann <ahofmann@uni-bremen.de>
Date: Fri, 1 Sept 2000 15:55:12
Subject: Final
```

```
Dear Miss Finch,
You are a laugh! I just can't resist writing to
```

you one last time because you really have no idea at all about Marc and me. You are jealous, spiteful and mean. You want to destroy something when you don't even have the slightest idea what it is. If it was not so evil it would be funny. What is Marc to you? A boyfriend? Well, then, go ahead and tell him because, rest assured, he has no idea of it.

Perhaps we can now end this farce.

Look for another enemy because I have no time for you and I have no fun with my horse, as you keep saying, because my horse is sick and I am very worried. So go ahead and rejoice, as this is something you always wanted to hear from me. I AM VERY UNHAPPY BECAUSE MY LOVELY HORSE IS SICK AND I HAVE NO MONEY TO PAY THE VET! Suits you well, doesn't it?
FH

@ @ @

"What do you mean, you forgot?" Ellie seized the envelope from her mother's hand, her heart pounding as she saw the French stamp and recognised the familiar slanting scrawl. "This is my personal mail – you have no right to . . ."

"Elinor, for goodness sake!" Her mother ran a hand wearily

through her hair. "I have rather more important things on my mind than acting as postman."

She flung a tea towel at Ellie. "Besides," she added, "had you done as I asked and cleared up the kitchen you would have found it for yourself, stuck behind the toaster."

She gestured impatiently at the pile of dishes stacked on the draining-board. "It's time you started pulling your weight around here."

Ellie hurled the tea towel on to the table and glared at her mother. "Oh, that's right – have a go at me as usual! And why can't Becky do it? She's hardly incapable of drying up a few dishes at ten years old, is she? Why does it always have to be me?"

Even as she asked the question, Ellie knew the answer. Becky was the favourite, Becky was the one everybody felt sorry for. "Isn't she a darling?" relatives would murmur. "And so plucky, after all she's been through."

And although they never said it, Ellie could tell from the sidelong glances that she was the person everyone blamed for what had happened.

"Becky has enough on her plate," said her mother briskly, "and besides, you have just had a month's holiday in France. I seem to remember you saying that if only you could go, you'd do chores for evermore."

Ellie said nothing. She could hardly deny it – she would have promised her mother the moon if it meant getting away from home for four whole weeks. It wasn't that she didn't love her mum and sister; it was just that every day there was something to remind her, something to make the guilt dig deeper. Seeing Becky struggling to catch up with schoolwork, watching as she looked longingly at miniskirts in the window of New Look, or seeing her sitting on the sidelines at her school sports day – and knowing that it was all because of Ellie.

But it wasn't just me, was it? Ellie thought furiously. If Dad hadn't been . . . but no. It was pointless to think about it. She was the one who had seized Becky's hand; she was the one who had dragged her off across the park, down the hill, on to the towpath by the canal. If she hadn't done that, Becky would still be running and jumping and playing netball with her mates. If it hadn't been for me.

"Did you hear what I said?" Her mother's voice interrupted Ellie's thoughts. Mrs Finch looked tired – tired and drawn – but then, she often looked like that those days. What with all the worry about Becky, and trying to hold down two jobs after Dad got made redundant, Mum didn't seem to have time for much fun any more.

Ellie glanced down at the letter in her hand and suddenly felt charitable. She had her letter from Marc and what did Mum have?

"Now look," continued her mother, "I have to fetch Becky – you know how upset she gets if I'm late. And I expect this kitchen to be spotless when I get back. And your school uniform ironed ready for the start of term. OK?"

"OK," nodded Ellie, her fingers still caressing the airmail envelope. "I promise."

Her mother smiled and ruffled her hair. "Good," she said. "That's more like it."

She opened the kitchen door, paused and turned to face Ellie.

"And I'm sorry about forgetting your letter," she said. "It's just that I've got so much on my mind, what with Dad and . . ."

Ellie's stomach lurched. "Dad hasn't . . . ?"

Her mum shook her head. "No. Dad hasn't been in touch. Not yet."

Ellie struggled not to let the relief show on her face.

"But he will soon," her mother continued brightly. "I just know he will. And then we can all get back to normal."

"Normal! Us? Get real, Mum!" The words were out before Ellie had the chance to swallow them.

"Ellie!" her mother shouted, and then took a deep breath. "Look, love, it's not Dad's fault." She bit her lip. "I mean, this only happens when everything gets on top of him. You mustn't blame him."

Ellie swallowed hard. Oh no, I mustn't blame Dad. Because his disappearances, his mood swings, his drinking and everything that happens after it – they're all my fault too, aren't they?

"It all started after the accident . . ."

How many times had she heard her mother mutter those words to her best friend Isla?

"He's never been the same since that day . . . he adores Becky so . . ."

Ellie bit down on her thumbnail. I wish it had been me, and not Becky. He wouldn't have cared if it had been me. He wouldn't have these black moods if it was me in a wheelchair. I wish . . . Stop it! You know what will happen if you let yourself think like this. Blot it out. Come on. Start thinking nice thoughts.

Marc's letter. In your hand now. Full of loving messages. Because Marc really loves you. For you.

"You'd better get going, Mum!" Ellie said brightly. "Mustn't be late."

She waited until the front door had slammed and then ripped open the blue airmail envelope. Her fingers shook in eager anticipation as she pulled out the letter. Two pages! Two whole pages!

Ma chérie, she read. *Il fait seulement quatre jours que tu es partie et déjà je suis dévoré de désir de toi . . .*

A shudder of exquisite delight shot down Ellie's spine. Even without the help of her French dictionary, she could decipher the exhilarating fact that Marc was being eaten up with desire for her.

Est-ce que tu te souviens de la nuit dans le petit bois . . .

Did she remember the night in the little wood? How could she ever forget it? Her eyes scanned the page and she frowned in impatience. It was no good; she would have to get her dictionary. But wait – he'd switched into English further down the page.

So write to me soon, my little cabbage – each day I am looking at the mail to see is there a letter from you and each day I am distressed to see nothing. Already I think you have forgotten your Marc . . .

Your Marc! Ellie's heart soared. There was the proof, if ever she needed it. Which, of course, she didn't, because she had known all along that Freddie Hofmann was just making trouble. But still, it was good to see the words there on the page. Your Marc!

She ran up the stairs, two at a time, all thoughts of washing-up forgotten. She would write him a letter – no, better than that, she would e-mail him: let the passionate thoughts that were cascading through her mind spill out at once, so that he could read for himself just how she felt about him. The poor darling was clearly worried sick.

She flung open her bedroom door and grimaced. Even she had to admit that the room was a total tip. The floor was littered with clothes and books and half-finished holiday projects, all of which had to be completed by Monday's start of term. On the dressing-table, two apple cores and a banana skin lay in varying degrees of decomposition, and the bedside-table was cluttered with half-empty coffee cups. She picked one up and moved it to the dressing-table.

She'd clean up later.

Right now, she had more important things to attend to.

She switched on the computer.

My own darling Marc, Your letter arrived today and my heart is full of unspoken emotion.

(Very good.)

You must never think I have forgotten you. I yearn to be with you; I miss you so much and live on the memories of those magical moments when we held one another close and shared our innermost secrets.

Now what? She would have to translate all the French bits before she knew how to reply and then . . .

She was about to look up "*nous devons oublier*" when her computer flashed New Message!

She clicked her Inbox, eagerly anticipating yet more from Marc.

You are a laugh!

Friederike! Amazing! And this was the girl who was so adamant about not wanting to speak to her ever again.

Ellie grinned. She rather thought that Freddie would wish she'd kept quiet when Ellie told her the latest news. She couldn't pretend any longer to be Marc's special girlfriend, not once Ellie had given her a prècis of his letter.

Poor thing, she thought smugly, as she read the first paragraph of the e-mail. Me jealous? As if! What do I have to be jealous of? A horse-crazy girl with delusions of grandeur? Oh please!

. . . my horse is sick and I am very worried . . . I HAVE NO MONEY TO PAY THE VET! Suits you well, doesn't it?

Ellie frowned and read the paragraph again. And again. And it was the last five words that her eyes kept resting on. But it wasn't Freddie's horse that Ellie was remembering. It was a day long ago when her stomach kept lurching with fear and everyone seemed to be so angry.

"Becky is very sick . . . we are very worried . . . what do you mean, you can't remember? Suits you very well, doesn't it, just to forget? Suits you very well . . . suits you very well . . ."

Suddenly Ellie wasn't fourteen any more; she was ten. Ten years old and scared. Very, very scared. Everyone asking questions, everyone expecting answers. Not just Mum and Dad, but the policewoman with the curly hair and the doctor in the white coat. Becky lying so still in the big white hospital bed, much, much more still than she ever was when she was asleep in the room they shared at home. And Dad's voice saying the words over and over again: "What were you thinking of? If you had done as you were told, none of this would have happened. How could you?"

And then Mum sobbing, "And don't say you don't remember . . . suits you very well . . ."

Ellie bit her knuckle till it hurt. Stop it. Don't think about it.

Poor Freddie. If she felt about that horse as she had felt when she saw her sister . . . but that was ridiculous! It was a horse, for heaven's sake! True, she knew some people went dotty over animals but all the same . . . !

And besides, what was all this about not being able to afford the vet? Freddie, the girl who wore Calvin Klein jeans and Nike trainers, who treated the whole chalet to ice creams almost every day, pretending she was hard up? Anyone who owned a horse in the first place had to be well off – she knew that because after Becky began to get a bit better and went to Riding for the Disabled classes, her dad had enquired about buying her a pony. And had a blue fit when he found out the cost. That was when he had gone off for the first time and . . .

Ellie shook herself and hit the Reply to Sender button. Anything to keep her mind off the unthinkable.

To: Friederike Hofmann <ahofmann@uni-bremen.de>
From: Ellie Finch <elliefin@email.com>
Date: Sat, 2 Sept 2000 15:03:11
Subject: **Your horse**

Dear Freddie,

I'm sorry your horse is sick. Of course, you
won't believe me, because you are the sort of
person who always thinks the worst of everyone,
but actually it's true. Although it's the horse
I'm sorry for more than you. What's wrong with
it (aside from having you on its back every
day, that is)? I can't believe that you don't
have the money to call the vet – surely your
rich mummy and daddy will pay the bill? Or this
oh-so-perfect brother of yours, the one you kept
telling us adored you so much? Sad boy. Anyway,
even if they won't pay, you must have one of
those free vet services in Germany. We have one
here called the People's Dispensary for Sick
Animals, although I don't know if they do
horses. We took my sister's gerbil there once
when it swallowed a button.

What's wrong with me? thought Ellie, rereading the e-mail. In
a minute, I'll be getting all matey-matey with her. As if.

Anyway, I have to go and finish my e-mail to
Marc. Did I mention he had written? Two pages.

31

He misses me dreadfully, poor love. And yes,
since you ask, Marc is my boyfriend . . .

She paused and read the sentence out loud. "Marc is my boyfriend."

She smiled to herself. It sounded good. And it would make a wonderful talking point at school next week. Of course, Lisa, her best friend, knew already; she had been practising her mime by the lakeside that afternoon when Marc had kissed Ellie for the very first time. But even Lisa didn't know everything else that had happened. No one did. Yet.

So I suggest you devote your attentions to your
horse and accept the fact that Marc is mine and
mine alone. You will save yourself a lot of
trouble.
Ellie

PS Get that? He's mine!

There! She clicked on Send. Done!

Perhaps now Friederike would get the message. It was about time.

Ellie hoped her horse would be all right. Even someone like Freddie Hofmann didn't deserve two shocks in one day.

Ellie was just trying to work out what it was that Marc was saying they must forget (she'd just discovered that *oublier* meant forget) when the doorbell shrilled urgently. Mum forgotten her key again, no doubt. She sped downstairs and yanked open the front door. Standing on the doorstep was Lisa, her face flushed and her mahogany-brown hair hanging dishevelled over her shoulder. "I got the photos!" she panted, leaning against the doorpost. "The photos from camp – they're mega!"

"Wicked!" exclaimed Ellie, seizing her arm. "Come up to my room and show me – and while you're at it, you can do a spot of translating for me."

Lisa frowned and followed her up the stairs. "Don't tell me you've left your holiday assignment till now?" she gasped. "You'll never . . ."

Ellie smiled smugly. "Not that, silly!" she replied. "I've had a letter. From Marc." She pushed open the bedroom door and crossed to her desk.

"Oh, that!" said Lisa dismissively. "I got one too – I guess everyone did; the camp newsletter and an application form for next year, you mean?"

"No!" Ellie snapped. "Look!" She waved the pages in front of Lisa's face. Lisa's eyes sped over the writing with the expertise of one who always got straight A's for languages.

"Wow!" she said. "So that wasn't just one casual kiss I saw, then? Is this guy smitten or what?"

Ellie turned to her eagerly. "Really? See, I can only read bits of it – what does this bit say?"

Lisa peered at the page. "*We must forget all those things that made you so sad* . . . What things? What made you sad?"

Ellie swallowed. "Nothing, I . . ."

"Come to think of it," mused Lisa, "you did have a couple of down days in the middle of the second week. So loverboy lent you a shoulder to cry on, did he?"

Ellie fixed a broad grin on her face. "Yeah – well, you know how it is! It was only PMT but I couldn't tell him that, could I? He thought I was homesick."

"You? That's a laugh," grinned Lisa, flicking her hair behind her ears. "Anyway, do you want to see these photos or not?"

"Hang on!" cried Ellie. "Just read me the rest. What comes after forgetting what makes me sad?"

". . . *and think only about the next time we shall meet . . .* um . . . what's that word? – wherever! . . . *wherever that may be. It is the thought of this reunion and the imaginings of my lips on yours that brightens my lonely days, my little cabbage. With love, your Marc.*"

Lisa turned to her friend. "Well, you certainly made a hit there, didn't you?" she teased. "You and half a dozen others!"

Ellie frowned. "What do you mean?"

"Well, you know what he was like – always chatting up the girls, telling them how cute they were – the French are like that!"

"Oh, sure!" agreed Ellie, trying desperately to sound cool and confident. "He was paid to be nice to everyone, wasn't he? But him and me – that was different. He told me I was the most special thing that had ever happened to him."

Lisa opened her mouth, paused and then shrugged. "Well, I guess you must have something – this letter is dead romantic. Now – can I show you these photos?"

For the next ten minutes the girls pored over the pictures from camp, giggling at close-ups of their attempts to master water polo in the swimming pool, sighing longingly over scenes on the nearby beach and spluttering over a close-up of

Lisa blowing her saxophone for all she was worth. They were almost at the bottom of the pile when Lisa grabbed a couple of photographs and stuffed them into her shoulder bag.

"Hey!" cried Ellie, stretching out a hand. "I haven't seen those two."

"Oh – er, they were duds – overexposed!" babbled Lisa, pushing her hand away. "Listen, there's something I simply have to tell you. Only you have to promise not to tell anyone else at school."

"OK," nodded Ellie.

"No, promise," insisted Lisa.

"I promise," repeated Ellie dutifully. "What?"

"I'm in love," said Lisa.

Ellie burst out laughing.

"What's so funny?" demanded Lisa. "You're not the only one who's fanciable, you know."

Ellie grinned. "You make it sound like it's an event," she said. "Lisa, you are ALWAYS in love with someone or other. Duncan, Alex, Matthew – and that was just last term!"

Lisa tossed her head impatiently. "That was just kids' stuff," she replied. "Something to help me get through the tedium of Nambridge High! This is for real. His name's Jason."

"I hate that name!" Ellie had spat out the words before she realised it.

"Well, I like it!" retorted Lisa. "He's gorgeous, Ellie – tall, with these rippling muscles like the guys on 'Baywatch' and jet-black eyes. Only don't tell anyone – not yet."

"Why not?"

"If Mum and Dad get to hear about him, they'll kill me."

35

Ellie frowned. "Surely they're used to you going through all the boys in Year Ten, aren't they?"

Lisa chewed her lip. "The thing is," she said, "Jason's loads older than me – he's nineteen."

Ellie shrugged. "So is Marc – I prefer older men, they have more sophistication and fewer zits."

"Exactly!" agreed Lisa, "but to hear Mum talk, you'd think I was on the path to eternal ruin. *That Jason Hill's so arrogant, that Jason Hill thinks he's so clever* – she goes on and on and . . . Ellie, what's the matter?"

Ellie was standing stock still, staring at Lisa, her eyes widening by the moment. "Did you say Jason Hill?" The question came out as a croak.

Lisa nodded, giving a swoony smile. "Mmm," she sighed. "Mrs Lisa Hill – sounds good, eh?"

Ellie didn't laugh. She didn't even smile. She stood, clenching and unclenching her fists, staring at Lisa. "What does he look like?" she asked abruptly.

"I told you – tall, muscular . . ."

"What colour hair?"

"Blond – at the moment! He bleached it last week – it looks dead cool!"

It can't be him! thought Ellie. I mean, Jason's a common enough name and Hill – well, heaps of people have that surname. But Jason – the boy of her nightmares, the one whose actions had ruined her life – would be nineteen by now.

This was crazy! Jason Hill didn't live in Nambridge – Ellie and her family had moved there after it all happened, to get away from the memories. She was being stupid.

"So," she said, trying desperately to sound laid-back, "where did you meet him?"

Lisa grinned. "My brother dragged him back home – they met at some gig at Daniel's college. Jason's new – he's moved here from Brighton. Hey, didn't you use to live down there?"

Ellie's knees were giving way beneath her. It was him. She just knew it was.

She sank down on to her desk chair, her hand clamped to her mouth as if the gesture would stop the feeling of nausea that was rising in her throat.

"But anyway," said Lisa, turning back to the letter, "enough about my love life! We have to decide what you must write back to the wonderful Marc!"

But suddenly even returning Marc's protestations of undying love seemed unimportant.

Jason Hill was in town. And Dad might come home at any moment.

The nightmare was going to start all over again. Ellie just knew it was.

@ @ @

Friederike shut the bathroom door behind her.

Nothing.

Still nothing.

Not even a tiny spot of red on her knickers.

She groaned inwardly. PLEASE, this must not happen. PLEASE, this must not happen. PLEASE, this must not happen.

The same sentence was repeating itself again and again in her numb brain like a mantra.

Still in a trance, she went downstairs and into her father's study. It was empty – no screen flickering, no voice humming to classical music as was usual when he was not away on one of his business trips.

Strange. He was at home – as she had dashed out to school that morning, she had seen his car in front of the garage.

So where was he?

Obviously not in his study – unless he was crouching on the floor behind his huge desk. Feeling faintly ridiculous, Rieke peered around its corner. Nobody.

So where was he?

She went to the bookcase at the far side of the room, where the dictionaries, lexicons and encyclopaedias were stacked. No novels here in Paps' private room: those were in the sitting-room, in Mammi's room and even in the dining-room, because this was a book-loving family. At least it used to be when all her brothers lived here.

Where was the right volume? N . . . O . . .

Ah, here. M.

Rieke leafed through the pages until she came to the word she was searching for. There it was: Menstruation.

Aha – *periodical recurrence of the monthly . . .*

She knew all that. This was not what she wanted to look up. Everybody of her age knew what menstruation was. She first had hers three – no, three and a half – years ago. It belonged to The Facts of Life, as Mammi had then explained to her, nothing to be afraid of, nothing to be ashamed of.

Rieke remembered that talk with longing. Mammi had congratulated her for being a real woman, although a very young one. Even if Rieke now had all the proper installations to enable her to have a child of her own it would be better to wait some years, wouldn't it? Still plenty of time for that, when she had a good relationship with the prospective father, a job, a perspective on life . . .

Rieke remembered the words her mother had used to convince her to take no risks, to protect herself against any disruption of her happy life as a teenager . . .

Happy life? Oh yeah! Wonderful!

I would love to wait. I would love to wait. I would love to wait . . .

There – she was on another mantra. Her world seemed to be full of mantras right now, as if by conjuring and repeating important words she could order reality to conform with her wishes.

She read on. Of course, but OF COURSE! There it was: teenagers could have irregular periods because of their still irregularly-functioning hormones; changes in the climate could be responsible too, or psychological stress – well, there it was.

Of course, she had any amount of stress: travel stress – surely a bus trip across half of Europe was considered stress?; stress with that stupid girl in England, who boasted that she was Marc's girlfriend and who kept sending mean messages; stress with Merlin being sick and stress with finding money for the vet.

Rieke breathed deeply. She pulled herself upright and felt a big weight gliding from her shoulders. Of course it was all that stress! So nothing to worry about.

Get on with your life, then, and stop being frightened! she admonished herself. She closed the book and put it back on the shelf.

Thank you, book, you have helped me greatly.

Then her thoughts returned to her absent father. Perhaps she could ask him for the money for the vet? Rieke made a tour of the house but, as she had thought, she was completely alone.

She went into the kitchen to make herself a big sandwich. Funny how hungry she always was since her return from France! As if she had to make up for the loss of Marc, the sun, the lake and the fun by stuffing herself with everything the fridge offered.

But then she saw the note on the little blackboard which hung beside the fridge:

FAMILY CONFERENCE TOMORROW EVENING
AT 8 O'CLOCK.
ANTON, FELIX AND JOHANNES ARE COMING TOO.
KISS, MAMMI

Hey, this was a surprise. So tomorrow the old rites would be re-established and there would be a family conference again, just like in the good old days.

Rieke smiled to herself while cutting thick slices from the big brown loaf and spreading creamy yellow butter on it. She thought about the times when they all had sat round the big kitchen table with a real agenda and democratic voting about where they would go for their holidays, and whether Johannes was allowed to take up judo lessons as well as karate, and who should weed the flower-beds, and who was supposed to vacuum the carpets on Friday . . .

She took an enormous bite from her salami sandwich and wondered about the last time they had met for a family conference. Must have been nearly a year ago, when Johannes moved out to study in Freiburg and Felix and Basti had fought over the question of who would move into Johannes' room. Yes, that was the last time.

Rieke chewed and thought about the reason why Mammi wanted another conference. And with Anton and Johannes, too. It was odd — what was there to be discussed any more? The boys went on holiday wherever they wanted, and even when she herself had been planning to spend those weeks at Lac Léon, nobody had been asked. It had been decided by Mammi.

So why have a conference now? Perhaps she could ask for money then — her big brothers might help her convince Paps and Mammi that a horse needed the best treatment it could get. And then, they might not. She was the only one with a horse and they had always teased her about being hopelessly spoiled by ageing parents — "*You know something, Rieke, when we were as old as you are now, we had to do the washing-up every day, and we had to clean our rooms weekly, and . . .*" blah blah.

As if she had wished to be a last child! And an only daughter, come to that.

She frowned as she climbed to her room, taking two steps at a time and devouring the rest of her sandwich in huge bites.

Well then, Maths was waiting – they had a test next week. But . . . Marc might have sent a sweet little message . . . And before she could stop herself, Rieke was at her screen, getting into the Internet: there was something waiting for her.

Ellie Finch! Again! No! Definitely no, she would close the connection and start with Maths – but contrary to her intention the message materialised on the screen and she couldn't help but read . . .

Dear Freddie, I'm sorry your horse is sick. Rieke read, and looked again. It couldn't be, could it? Ellie didn't mean that, surely – Rieke read on. Ah, but no, there it was – your rich mummy and daddy . . . this oh-so-perfect brother . . . no, nothing had changed. Ellie was still her hateful self, nothing to be grateful for. Although that mention of those free vet services they had in England sounded almost like concern, and that swallowed button – that was funny – but . . . Girl, get real! Rieke thought. This is Ellie, the menace, the liar, the stealer of boyfriends and supposed rival.

She thought some moments, then started typing:

To: Ellie Finch <elliefin@email.com>
From: Friederike Hofmann <ahofmann@uni-bremen.de>
Date: Sat, 2 Sept 2000 13:08:56
Subject: **Leave me alone!**

Hello Ellie,
We don't have that service here in Germany.
Everything is more or less private insurance

and so terribly expensive that even so-rich mummies and daddies are not eager to pay the instalments. Whatever gave you the idea we were German billionaires? And Bill Gates is not my relative, whatever you were told. The cure for Merlin is not too expensive, but somehow since my return from France my mother gets nervous whenever money is mentioned and I haven't found out yet how I'm supposed to take care of Merlin without a pfennig.

Anyway, stop gibbering about Marc - people don't BELONG to other people, that is plain stupid. I don't know why you still keep insisting that he is your boyfriend. Didn't you know that he and I had a full-blown romantic love story? With secret meetings at the lakeside and sailing trips in his friend's boat (when everyone thought we were rehearsing my lines); that we even spent some nights in a shed in the woods, which belongs to the camp but is hardly ever used? It was when I came home to our bungalow those nights that I found you sweating and mumbling in your bed and that's how I know you rarely slept well. So you could not have been soooo awfully happy right then, could you?

The love between Marc and me is the most beautiful thing that ever happened in my whole life . . .

Her fingers didn't move on. Yes it was, she thought defiantly. It was so beautiful that certainly nothing ugly could happen because of it . . . could it?

. . . and this is why I hate your lying and telling stories of relationships which never existed. I don't ask you to stop that, because I know you well enough to be absolutely sure that this would be the best way of tempting you to carry on with your fibs. So I tell you very simply the truth: Marc and I love each other, and he told me so many, many times - which are my most treasured memories of those summer weeks, and I will not have them smeared by your claims and half-truths. Of course Marc was nice to you as he was to everybody, but it is me he loves.

And I cannot forget those times for one second, even if I wanted to – which I don't, Rieke thought unhappily.

So let it be, Ellie, will you? You can't change what we had. Goodbye.
Rieke

Rieke swallowed because she felt like crying. She moved the mouse to Send and got up from her desk. She didn't only feel like crying, she felt sick.

This . . . did not mean . . . surely not. It must have been the

44

sandwich, of course – she'd gobbled it down much too fast, this was the reason she felt so queasy.

But while trying to reassure herself that everything was all right, she sensed again that fear like a big black cannonball deep down in her stomach, making her legs wobbly and her mind dizzy.

But everything's OK, it was just the sandwich, she thought again as she ran to the bathroom and vomited into the toilet.

When the heaving had stopped, she washed her face and her hands and brushed her teeth. Then she looked into the mirror and eyed her pale image.

No, it can't be, she decided. This is not possible. Because nothing happened which could . . . Even if there had been that one night when she fell asleep.

But Marc had been so considerate and sweet – he even had a numb arm when she woke up later, because he hadn't dared to pull it from under her head . . .

There could have been nothing else. Of course, nothing had happened. So, this can't happen to me.

But Rieke cried. Heavy tears rolled down her cheeks. Angrily she brushed them away.

Everything was all right! She would concentrate on the tasks that lay before her. Do her Maths homework. Go and look after Merlin. Write an e-mail to Marc. Look forward to the family conference.

What was that going to be about, anyway?

"Ellie! Have you been listening to a single word I've said?" Lisa poked Ellie in the ribs and gestured towards the computer screen.

"I thought you were supposed to be in love with this guy," she sighed. "Here I am, using all my creative genius and linguistic skills to compose the love-letter to end all love-letters and you're stuck there, staring out of the window with a face like doom! What's the matter?"

Ellie gave herself a shake and forced a smile on to her lips. "Sorry," she murmured. "Just daydreaming." She could hardly tell Lisa that, far from thinking of Marc, the only images in her head had been Jason Hill's face that day – that arrogant look, the way their eyes met in that instant before . . .

"Ellie?" Lisa peered at her friend. "Are you OK?"

"Fine," said Ellie. Just stop looking back, she ordered herself silently. Just think about Marc. "Read it to me," she said, wondering how she'd got herself into this, and whether she should tell Lisa about her own half-written reply.

"*My dearest darling Marc. I, too, dream of the day when I can once again lie in your arms, feel the tender touch of your lips against mine, thrill to the pressure of your firm body against my breasts and . . .*"

"Lisa!" Ellie felt her cheeks burn. "You can't!"

"Can't what?"

"Write that – you know – all that stuff!"

Lisa gave her friend a withering look. "So are you telling me that none of that happened? That it was just the usual kids' stuff – hand-holding, the odd peck on the cheek, a little goodnight hug? Is that what you are saying?"

Ellie thought back to those long, warm evenings by the lake, the walks in the woods, the snatched moments when they sat, swinging their legs, on the end of the wooden jetty. There was more than that, wasn't there? He had kissed her passionately on the lips, he had stroked her hair and rocked her gently in his arms, his hands straying to the buttons on her polo shirt . . .

"Of course not!" she retorted, desperately searching for the right words. "But I mean, putting it down in black and white . . . well . . ."

"Ellie Finch! Do you want Marc to see you as a sensuous, sexy woman – or as some dippy teenager who hasn't a clue what it's all about?"

Lisa glared at Ellie and without waiting for an answer continued, ". . . *and know that you are mine and I am yours for ever. The only sadness I have is the sadness of separation from you . . .*"

Lisa grinned. "I'm good at this, aren't I? That's what comes from being in love."

"Mmm," murmured Ellie, somewhat unenthusiastically. If Lisa really was dead keen on Jason, she would be sure to drag him around everywhere with her, which meant that sooner or later, Ellie would meet him. And if it was THE Jason, he would recognise her. And that didn't bear thinking about.

"So?" enquired Lisa, hitting the full stop button with a flourish. "Let's send it!"

Ellie swallowed and thought fast. "I'll do it later," she gabbled.

"No, now!" insisted Lisa. "You have to keep passions running high – I read it in this book *The Real Truth About Love, Sex and Everything*. It's dead good – I'll lend it to you if you like."

The real truth. That was a laugh. No one told the real truth about anything – they just told you what they wanted you to know and kept the rest hidden.

"OK, thanks," Ellie said automatically. "And don't worry, I'll send the e-mail – only Mum goes ballistic if I don't wait until cheap rate. She says I'm lucky that they were able to get me my own computer while Dad still had a job, and I have to be responsible – you know the kind of thing . . ."

Lisa nodded knowingly. "I'm never going to get like that," she said, fiddling with the mouse. "You know, obsessed about material things like phone bills and the price of trainers."

At that moment there was a loud beep from the machine. Lisa jumped and dropped the mouse. "Hey – what happened? I didn't touch anything – honest!"

Ellie grinned. "It's just saying I've got a new message," she said, pointing to a small flashing envelope in the top right-hand corner of the screen. She leaned in front of Lisa, went into the Inbox and gasped.

"Not loverboy again?" enquired Lisa.

Ellie shook her head, zapped the e-mail in the holding folder, and shut down the computer. "No," she said hastily.

"So who was it?" demanded Lisa, who liked to know every detail of her friends' lives.

Ellie was saved from telling a lie by a loud screech. "ELINOR! Get down these stairs this instant!"

Ellie blanched. Mum was back. And the dishes were still on the draining-board, and the ironing-board was still in the cupboard.

Footsteps thundered up the stairs and the bedroom door was flung open. "Can you not be trusted to carry out the simplest task?" shouted Mrs Finch, her face flushed with annoyance. "I have just about had enough of your total disregard for . . . Oh! Lisa. I didn't see you there."

"I was just off, Mrs Finch," said Lisa in the sort of simpering voice she used for irate Maths masters. "I was just showing Ellie the photos from camp and hearing all about her love . . ."

"So you'd better go!" interjected Ellie hastily. "I must help Mum." She almost pushed Lisa down the stairs and out of the front door. "Don't mention Marc!" she hissed through gritted teeth. "Otherwise she'll start checking my e-mails and then all hell will break loose."

"OK," said Lisa amiably. "Good, isn't it? You and me – we've both got secret lovers. Soooo romantic!" She sighed. "Pity Marc's not over here," she added. "Then we could go out in a foursome. Him and you, me and Jason."

"Mmmm," said Ellie, who couldn't think of anything worse. "Must dash – see you!"

It wasn't until fifteen minutes later, when she was standing at the ironing-board, absent-mindedly pressing her school skirt and trying not to listen as her mother went on and on about responsibilities and how the world didn't owe her a living, that an astonishing thought struck Ellie. The e-mail that had arrived just before Lisa left had been from Freddie. That wasn't astonishing at all. But what was surprising was Ellie's determination that Lisa shouldn't see the message.

Freddie's *my* friend, she had thought as she hastily shut down the computer. Which was, of course, a load of nonsense. Freddie was her deadliest enemy, a man-stealing, conniving, self-opinionated little madam! So why, Ellie asked herself, slipping her skirt on to a hanger and flinging a crumpled school shirt on to the ironing-board, can't I wait to get back upstairs and read what she says? How can I possibly care about her ramblings over some dumb horse or her imagined love affair with Marc?

And, most oddly of all, why do I have this overpowering urge to tell her about Jason Hill? Why? It doesn't make any sense. I hate the girl.

I do, really.

It was hours before Ellie could shut herself in her bedroom and switch on her computer. Once she had finished the ironing her mum decided that she should help Becky with her physiotherapy exercises; when that was done, Ellie's grandmother dropped in, and despite saying she could only stay a second, managed to stay for ages – while telling Ellie that she should get her hair cut shorter, stop biting her fingernails and abandon cropped tops in favour of nice little woollen cardigans. Then her mum suggested they should all go for a nice walk in the park. It was only by pretending that she had to check on her assignments for school that Ellie had managed to make her escape at all.

She shut the bedroom door and with fingers that, to her surprise, were trembling slightly, she clicked into her e-mail folder. There it was – the e-mail from Freddie. She ran her eyes over the lines of type.

. . . since my return from France my mother gets nervous whenever money is mentioned . . .

I can identify with that, thought Ellie. The last four years had been one long session of scrimping and saving; it was only because her mum had sold some old jewellery that Ellie had been able to go to camp in Lac Léon in the first place – that, and the fact that her dad had added fifty pounds because he was so glad to see the back of her. Sometimes she wished she didn't have to think of him as "my dad": after all, he wasn't, was he? And that was half the problem. Becky was his – his very own little princess, he called her. And Ellie? Ellie was just Sheila's kid – the child he had taken on in order to marry the woman he professed to love.

Forcing her thoughts away from all these things, Ellie turned her attention back to Freddie's e-mail. Uh-oh! She thought it had been too good to last! Here she was, ranting and raving again about Marc. What was this?

. . . he and I had a full-blown romantic love story? . . . secret meetings . . . sailing . . . nights in a shed . . .

No! That couldn't be! That shed was their place – hers and Marc's. He had taken her there the evening she got a splinter in her foot. He'd sat her down on the dilapidated old sofa inside the door, gently lifted her foot and kissed the sore place. And then he had kissed her ankle, and her shin, and then her knee, all the time telling her how sweet she was, and how desirable, and how glad he was that she had come into his life. He wouldn't have taken Freddie there! She must have made it up.

But she wouldn't, Ellie thought miserably. Even Freddie, with her overactive imagination, wouldn't think to invent that. Unless – maybe she found the shed on one of the long rambles in the woods and maybe she thought how cool it would be to have it as a secret hideaway and then invented this rubbish about Marc loving her.

That would be it.

But no matter how many times Ellie tried to convince herself, she couldn't make herself wholly believe it.

Of course, even if it was true, Freddie couldn't possibly say that Marc was hers and hers alone, because Ellie had been kissed in that same shed, and had lain in Marc's arms and . . . well, no. She hadn't actually done anything else because every time Marc got mega-affectionate she found herself leaping to her feet and claiming that she had a rehearsal to go to or a swimming practice or mime class. Now she wished she had been more sophisticated, more laid-back – more experienced. What if Freddie had been? What if Marc and Freddie . . . ?

But no. That was crazy. Freddie might be a stuck-up so-and-so, but she wasn't that much of a fool.

Was she?

There was only one way to find out. Ellie began typing.

Hi, Freddie!
So you went to the shed with Marc, did you?
The shed with the broken window, and the green
door with peeling paint, and the battered red
sofa inside? Well, so did I, and more than
once, I can promise you! And we didn't just

sit and talk, either! So don't start thinking
that you are Marc's one and only love; what he
and I had was a mature relationship. I guess
with you he was just trying to be kind and
make you feel at home.

She stopped typing and reread the words. She was being
stupid. She knew that wasn't true. Maybe – just maybe – she
should say what she was really thinking.

Unless he was two-timing us. Unless he was
saying all the same things to you as he said to
me. Not that I believe that is true for a
moment, considering the letter I received from
him today. He's missing me so much - says he's
quite overcome with passion for me. And he
sounds pretty committed to me! Like me to quote
you a bit? Well, get this!
    ". . . *it is the thought of this reunion and
the imaginings of my lips on yours that
brightens my lonely days, my little cabbage.*"
And in case you don't know, *petit choux* is a
term of endearment in France. So there!

Again Ellie reread what she had written. And funnily enough,
she didn't get the satisfaction from her harsh words that she
had expected to get. Would Freddie feel as she did now? – a
sort of sick, hollow pain in the pit of her stomach – and
would she, too, be upset at the possibility (only a very vague

possibility, of course) that Marc's love was not all it seemed? Maybe she should write something nice to end with.

Is your horse better today? I know what it's like to have mothers wittering on about money; mine never stops. I guess they've had to spend so much on Becky since . . . (She crossed out the last word.) . . . recently that there's nothing left to fall back on. Surely your parents wouldn't let a dumb animal suffer just for material gain? Couldn't you say that to them - make them feel guilty? It usually works.
   By the way, my friend Lisa (remember her - the one with the saxophone and the long brown hair?) - well, she got her pictures back from camp and they are really funny. There aren't any of you - not that I want one, of course. But there are some cool ones of Marc and me.

OK, so it's a lie, but not a really big one. Ellie sighed. She wished she hadn't thought of Lisa, because thinking of her made her think of Jason Hill and that was bad news. Her fingers hovered over the keyboard and she almost began to tell Freddie the whole saga. But that was crazy! The girl was a pain – no way was she going to give her anything else to gloat over.

Must dash - hope you get the money out of your parents.
Love Ellie

She clicked on Send and sent the message winging on its way. Then sat bolt upright. *Love Ellie!?* I didn't actually write *love*, did I? she thought, horrified. To that jerk? Ye gods, I must be losing it!

Tutting to herself, Ellie checked the Inbox.

But there was nothing from Marc.

Perhaps she should send that sexy message that Lisa had composed. But then again . . .

She'd do it tomorrow. By tomorrow she would have heard from Marc. She'd wait till then.

@ @ @

There! A letter for her on the table in the hall. Eagerly Rieke ripped open the envelope and unfolded the sheet of paper. She squinted at the still unfamiliar handwriting. These French seemed to teach another set of letters in school . . .

Ma petite sorcière,
Tu m'as complètement enchanté. Tu me manque pire qu'avant. I miss you so much! Je suis rentré à Paris pour travailler quelques semaines avant de commencer l'université. Just imagine: je suis le garçon dans un bistro pas loin du Boul Mich. Mais je ne peux pas me concentrer sur mes clients ou sur mes livres parce que je pense toujours à toi . . .

So – she was a little witch and had enchanted him – lovely! And he still missed her – but why the phrases in English?

Rieke read about his daily routine and the friends he had met again after the long holiday until the final avowal of love and papery kisses, and frowned. All right, so he missed her very much, nice to hear – nice to read, come to that. But why the English sentences strewn in? Marc and she had never talked in English – it was not a first language for either of them, and her French had been good enough to understand his murmured caresses and pledges of love, and what she had not known she had quickly learned. So why now these English words?

She reread the letter, puzzled a little longer and put the sheet back in the envelope. Strange.

Until four days ago this letter would have beamed her on to cloud nine; she would have felt perfectly happy and secure in the knowledge that her love for Marc and his for her had not just been a summer flirtation, but a real emotional involvement – not puppy love, but grown-up love.

But now as she waited impatiently for her period, which was overdue by a week, it seemed almost irrelevant. She had always been so punctual! Of course, all her apprehensions were just a laugh. Nothing had happened, nothing at all which could prevent her from getting her period! It was only – well, psychological, or travelogical, or whatever-ical.

But despite her brave admonitions to herself Rieke was sick with fear, and the queasy feeling she'd had in the mornings since had not helped to make her feel better.

She sighed, stuffed the envelope into her back pocket and

went to get her bike to cycle to Merlin. When she turned round the garage corner, she saw her father just getting into his car.

"Hi, Paps, where are you going?" she yelled.

He lowered the window and said, "Don't make such a fuss! I'm driving to Bremen for a meeting. See you later, alligator!" he added.

"In a while, crocodile," she answered automatically to their old parting joke, while wondering why he was dressed rather formally. Perhaps he was meeting with new clients? He wasn't laughing as normal when he spoke – he looked troubled.

He waved to her and drove off and she pedalled the five minutes to Farmer Mertens' stable. When she entered the saddleroom she found him talking to the vet, Dr Schütz.

"Ah, there she is!" Dr Schütz exclaimed. "Good news for you, young lady! It was the parasites as we had thought, nothing worse. So Merlin should be OK in a week and you can ride again soon, when he's had his dose of medicine and a bit of extra food during the next few days."

"Great!" Rieke felt a big weight slipping from her heart.

"Take it easy at the beginning, only half an hour of riding," added Farmer Mertens. "Let him build up his strength again."

Rieke beamed at the two men. Wow! That was the best news she'd had all day. "Have you treated him already, Dr Schütz? And when will I get the bill?"

The old man chuckled. "Not so fast, not so fast – all in good time. Yes, he got his dose. And I will come back in two days and make sure he is all right. And the bill – well, I wouldn't worry, if I were you. I'll send it to your mother as usual."

"Thanks a lot!" And then Rieke was running towards the paddock, where Merlin now stood with the farmer's horses in an open stable. She called him and when he came, she hugged him, and talked to him and fed him some titbits. What a beautiful horse he was with the white star between his huge brown eyes!

Rieke spent longer with her horse than she had planned, so it was rather late when she got home. Her mother was in the kitchen.

"Coming, Mammi!" she shouted, running up to her room. She threw her clothes on the floor and changed into clean jeans and a sweatshirt. Still time enough to look if there was . . .

No! She was not really interested in what that mean liar had to say! But still . . .

And before having decided if she was interested or not, Rieke had switched on her computer and was going on-line.

There it was! Mail!

. . . shed with the broken window, and the green door with peeling paint, and the battered red sofa . . .

But that was THEIR shed, Marc's and hers! How could Ellie know about it? Surely she must have spied on them, followed them when they met and found out about the shed . . .

But no! Ellie might be a complete pain and difficult to deal with but she had not been devious, she hadn't been sly . . . or had she?

Oh no, surely not – that was impossible! How could she even think of something so absolutely horrid!

Rieke read mechanically through the message, but her mind was repeating two-timing, two-timing and suddenly she felt sick again. She rushed to the bathroom and knelt in front of the loo, but only dry rasping sounds came from her throat.

She felt cold sweat on her front, got up and washed her face slowly, dried it and looked in the mirror.

Two-timing, two-timing . . .

It hurt. It hurt so much.

Rieke went downstairs to help her mother with the cooking. Inge Hofmann was standing at the sink peeling potatoes.

"What is this family conference all about, Mammi? And when will the boys be coming?"

Her mother looked at her watch. "Well, I've told them we will start at eight. So I guess they will arrive then."

"And what is so important to bring them all home?" Rieke opened the fridge and poured herself a glass of lemonade.

"Please, I don't want to tell everything twice, so wait till they're all here, OK?" Her mother's voice sounded weary, and when she touched her cheek with the back of her hand she seemed to brush away invisible tears.

Rieke was shocked. Up to that moment she had thought about the family conference as a nostalgic joke, but suddenly it seemed as if there was something really important going on. It felt as if some sort of Sword of Damocles was hanging over them. She shuddered and concentrated on washing the salad, chopping the onions and making salad dressing – nice, reassuring, everyday activities which perhaps could hold at bay what was looming.

When Basti came down to lay the table, Felix and Johannes had already arrived and were talking about the work they'd been doing during the university summer break.

Just like Marc, thought Rieke, and shivered. Marc, who could not concentrate on his job as a waiter because of her, but who used English words in a letter . . .

Two-timing, two-timing . . .

I'm definitely some sort of mantra person, Rieke thought, and tried to listen to the stories her brothers were telling. Anything to get away from those painful thoughts and to make Mammi laugh and push off the thing that had brought them together tonight.

They had already finished the salad when Anton arrived. As if by tacit agreement, they all avoided asking their mother the reason for the conference during the meal, but exchanged news as they wolfed down the boeuf bourguignon she had cooked – one of the favourite family dishes. Only when the table was cleared and they all sat down again were they silent, waiting for her to begin.

Anxiously Rieke glanced at the empty chair at the end of the table, opposite her mother. How come Paps was not there? Why did he leave the task of talking to their children to Mammi? Did he know what was going on? Did it even concern him?

Her mother cleared her throat. "Well, thank you, every-body, for coming. I only wish there could have been a nicer reason for this get-together. But, to cut a long story short, we are really deeply in trouble. Financially and otherwise. Your father has started to gamble heavily and we are deeply in debt."

Inge ignored the different exclamations of disbelief and surprise and carried on.

"Fortunately this house does not belong to the bank any longer as all the mortgage is paid, and it is in my name. But as we never made a marriage contract, under state law half of everything I own belongs to your father. And now it does not belong to him any more because he has gambled it away."

"Stop, Inge, please stop for a second!" Anton interrupted. "How long has this gone on? Why didn't you put a stop to it earlier?"

"That shows you don't know a thing about compulsive habits." His mother smiled sadly. "Of course I knew that he always liked a bet at the races or to go to the Spielcasino once in a while. But now it seems to have become almost daily, and he is already barred from the Bremen Spielcasino because of a little scandal he was involved in, so he now goes to Travemünde or Bad Zwischenatin or even to casinos further away."

"But when did it change?" Johannes asked, stupefied. "When did it become so bad?"

His mother shook her head. "I can't put my finger on it, but it seems to have become really bad during that time Rieke and I were in New York and he was living here with Sebastian."

"But, Basti, how . . . ?" Felix turned and glared at his younger brother.

"Hey – wait a minute!" Basti threw up his hands in a gesture of defence. "Most of the time I stayed with Till in Bremen – his parents invited me as they knew I was alone with Paps. Everyone knew that."

"Oh, Felix, stop that! I didn't mean to make Sebastian responsible for what happened," his mother smiled ruefully. "Perhaps I should have known that Jens would try to amuse himself with those things he likes best – and being a computer freak he has this weird idea that there exists a mathematical trick for winning at roulette – you know, trying to think out methods of number sequences and stuff like that."

Inge Hofmann looked around the table. "The thing is – nothing is helped by blaming him. What I want to do is minimise the damage. I have been to a lawyer and she has advised me to file for divorce."

"No!"

"How could you?"

"Impossible!"

"Terrible!"

When all her brothers had voiced their stupefaction, Rieke said into the ensuing silence, "So this is why he was dressed so formally."

Her mother glanced at her. "Yes, darling. You are not allowed to enter a Spielcasino in jeans."

"I wondered when he drove off today. He said he was going to a meeting – and I thought he meant his firm."

"More his gambling mates, I should think," Felix said dryly. "Well, Inge, tell us, what can we do to help you?"

"Right now I can't think of anything except your

understanding of the whole damned situation and your not blaming me for it." Inge Hofmann sighed deeply. "I have to work out the rest with my lawyer. The best I could think of ·was asking him if he would be willing to enter therapy – but he doesn't even want to speak of it. That is probably the worst part: he has no sense of reality any more. For him it is just an unfortunate episode which will soon be over. He is kidding himself, but there you are. When all this started I tried to learn as much as I could about addiction, and the books say that loss of reality is typical for addicts. And apparently this is how we should think of it: he is addicted to gambling and, like all addicts, is not totally responsible for what he is doing."

She sighed again. "I am not at all as open-minded and understanding as I would like to be; most of the time I would like to kick him where it hurts for doing this to himself and to us." She placed her hands on the table.

"But what does this mean? Do I have to give up Merlin?" asked Rieke in a small voice.

"Do I have to give up my studies?" asked Felix and Johannes simultaneously.

"Do you need money?" asked Anton, who was the only one who earned a regular salary as a dental assistant.

"No thank you, darling!" His mother reached out and patted his hand. "I still earn enough to keep our heads above water – that is not the point. A professor's salary is not bad. And you can keep your horse as long as I can afford to run the house. I still don't understand everything about the debts and how they affect me as well. This is something I have to find out in the next few days. But . . ."

Inge glanced at her children, one after the other. "I have to think about divorce, if this contract thing is not possible any more. To save the rest of what I own. And this is what really hurts."

She put her hands on her face, and Anton laid his arm round her shoulders. "It is stupid to tell you not to worry, because we are all worrying, but don't think too much about us, or how it would affect us. Think of yourself," he said.

"But . . . but . . . Papa . . ." Rieke stuttered, looking from Felix to Johannes and to Basti. "I don't want him to leave – I don't . . ."

And suddenly she started to cry. She put her arms on the table and buried her head in them. Then she cried her heart out. Papa a gambler. Mammi thinking of divorce. Marc's betrayal; her stupid period not coming; that Ellie making it all worse by jeering and lying – it was just too much.

Rieke cried till she had run out of tears. Mammi stroked her hair, Basti patted her arm, the three big brothers made soothing noises. Eventually she lifted her head and gratefully accepted a tea towel from Felix to clean her face and blow her nose.

"Anton, you go and get the good glasses from the dining-room cupboard," ordered their mother. "Felix, you go to the pantry and fetch a bottle of Rioja – no, better still, bring two bottles. Johannes and Basti, put the dishes into the dishwasher. I'm going to fetch candles, and Rieke, you look for matches."

With a grim look Inge mustered her children. "You know, we are all still alive and well, and that's what counts the most. So as we are finished with our business for tonight, let's start celebrating that we are together now, after such a long time. There are worse things than a father who spends more money than he has got."

"Boy, she's as tough as old boots," Felix said admiringly when their mother had left the kitchen. "Come on, everybody, let's have a party!"

When the alarm-clock rang the next morning, Rieke didn't know quite why she felt so light-hearted.

And as she remembered bit by bit what had happened yesterday evening she wondered more about this feeling – there was certainly no reason for happiness with a problem father like hers!

But on the other hand it had been good to have all her brothers back home again for once and they'd not treated her as a baby but as a grown-up. Maybe serious problems made you grow up faster. Or they made big brothers realise that their sister is not a little girl any more. Rieke smiled to herself, but when she swung her legs out of bed the terrible feeling came back. Again. She ran to the bathroom and vomited. She looked at her pale face in the mirror but her lips had no soothing answer for the anxious eyes.

Rieke dressed – even the word breakfast made her feel ill – and hurried to catch the school bus.

"You what?" Anna stared so hard at Rieke that her eyes almost popped out of their sockets.

"I didn't get my period."

"Are you ill?"

65

"Only in mind," Rieke answered cryptically and looked at the sandwich her friend was holding, waiting for the queasy feeling to start. Surprisingly, it didn't.

"Well, what reason . . . ? Oh no!"

"That's what I say all the time – oh no!" Rieke smiled with false courage.

"But how . . . ?" Anna rolled her oggling eyes to heaven. "This is a miracle. A virgin pregnancy." She grabbed Rieke's arm and drew her nearer. They were standing in their favourite corner of the school yard and nobody was near them, but she whispered nevertheless. "Or did you?"

"Did I what?"

"I mean you and Marc – did you?"

"Of course not!" Rieke retorted indignantly.

"Then why the fuss?" Anna bit into her sandwich and Rieke turned away. But still no queasy feeling.

"Why? Because . . . Oh, Anna, sometimes you just don't understand. I'm worried to death and all you can say is why the fuss!"

"But if you didn't do anything, what the hell are you worrying about?"

Yes, indeed. Why should I? Rieke thought to herself. So I won't any more. But then – what if . . . ? Rieke decided to close the subject. Sometimes even best friends didn't quite get it. And there was a limit to intimacies even between best friends – the thought of telling Anna about the catastrophe with Paps: a gambler who was ruining his family . . . no! That would never do! Some things you couldn't even tell your best friend.

Later that afternoon, having returned from visiting the convalescent Merlin, Rieke sat down at her desk and looked for a long time at her computer.

Should she?

Because she would explode if she could not talk about it.

Her oldest brothers had returned to the towns where they were working or studying and Basti was staying over in Bremen again.

Mammi was at the university and Paps – well, she wouldn't have known how to talk to him. Or what about. Everything was different now.

And in an odd way, maybe it would be easier to confide in someone who wasn't a friend – someone distant . . . So . . .

So Rieke started up her computer and went on-line.

Dear Ellie
Guess what happened in my oh-so-rich-and-beautiful family! You won't believe it, but perhaps you are the only one who can understand what it feels like if things go wrong.

She realised this had a double meaning and hastened to add the next words.

I don't mean our disastrous love life. I think about the time your friend Lisa told about the accident of this little sister of yours. I never understood what actually happened - Lisa clammed up when we asked questions - but it seemed really tragic. So you can understand maybe when I say that now I am dreadfully unhappy because my father is not the hero I always thought him to be. Instead he has done something absolutely terrible and I don't even know if I love him any more.

There, she thought to herself. The truth. But she wouldn't tell it all. If Ellie chose to make fun of her, she could not poke into an open wound. Better to stay safe.

I think this is the worst time I ever had in my life and even the memory of Marc doesn't help so much any more. I still can't get over your hint that he is perhaps two-timing us - he sent me a letter with an ENGLISH sentence between his French ones. By the way, I am not his little cabbage; he calls me his little witch. Which would you prefer? I like the witch better.

I don't know if you will answer this mail because I know I'm rambling on a bit but it was not so bad having had someone to write to now. Best wishes (if not for your love life in case it concerns a certain person)
Rieke

@ @ @

"So where the hell were you?" Lisa grabbed Ellie's arm as she burst through the locker-room door on Monday morning, just two minutes before the bell rang for morning registration. "I waited at the crossroads for ages!"

Ellie flushed and looked apologetic. "Sorry," she mumbled. "I got the bus."

"The bus!" Lisa exclaimed, looking as astonished as if her friend had admitted to arriving at school by flying saucer. "But we agreed – we cycle or we walk. No messing. This fitness campaign was your idea in the first place, remember?"

Ellie nodded ruefully. It had seemed important at the time; she had just discovered a dimple of cellulite on her right thigh. But she could hardly tell Lisa that the only campaign she was interested in right now was avoiding any possibility of bumping into Jason Hill. Just suppose she had cycled and met Lisa, and Jason had been with her and . . .

"So tomorrow we cycle, right?" demanded Lisa, raising her voice over the shrilling of the school bell.

"I thought," ventured Ellie tentatively, avoiding a straight answer, "that you might be walking with Jason – you know, on his way to college."

"Oh, I will be," replied Lisa airily as they clattered upstairs to registration, "but not till next week – college doesn't start till then. And no way would Jason get up in the mornings unless he really had to."

Ellie let out a sigh of relief. At least she had seven days to work out her tactics. Seven days to come up with a plan that would ensure that Jason Hill would never find out the identity of Lisa's best friend.

"Don't worry," grinned Lisa, squeezing Ellie's arm, "you don't have to wait that long to meet him. I'll drag him round to your place one evening and . . ."

"No!" The word was out before Ellie could stop it. "That is – it's difficult right now. Mum's decorating."

It was a bare-faced lie and she hated herself for saying it, but what choice did she have? If Jason Hill turned up on their doorstep, Mum would recognise him. And what if Dad was back by then? Not to mention how Becky would react. She had to stop it happening at all costs.

"So?" Lisa looked miffed. "She can't be doing the whole house in one go."

"No, but . . ."

"I get it!" retorted Lisa. "You're jealous!"

"Jealous?" Ellie frowned. "How do you work that out?"

"Because Marc is hundreds of miles away, and you can't see him – you can't bear for me to have romance on my doorstep."

"Oh, grow up!" The mixture of panic and worry made Ellie snap rather more than she had intended. "Why would I be jealous of you going out with a jerk like Ja . . ." She stopped, realising that she had said too much.

"What do you know about Jason? You've never set eyes on him. That just proves it – you're jealous!"

Lisa tossed her head and stormed off into the classroom.

Ellie pushed through the cluster of kids in the doorway and headed after her. "Lisa, wait!" She took a deep breath. "Sorry. I didn't mean it. I don't know what got into me. PMT, I guess. Sorry."

Lisa looked slightly mollified. "Yes, well . . ." she muttered. "I know what – how about you come over to my place on Wednesday? Jason's coming round and we could . . ."

"Lisa Farrell! Is it possible that you could stop talking – or is your tongue on automatic pilot?" Mrs Dunmore, the year tutor, glowered at Lisa from across the room as the class tittered in amusement. Ellie seized the opportunity to slip into a spare seat at the back of the room and busy herself with emptying her schoolbag.

Wednesday. She had to think up a good excuse by Wednesday. But how? Even if she managed it this time, Lisa wouldn't rest until she had shown off her precious Jason. And he'd be sure to recognise her; unlike some of her friends she had hardly changed in the four years since that fateful afternoon. Sure, she was taller; sadly she had even more freckles than when she was ten years old, but apart from that there was no difference. Even her hair was pretty much the same – a bit longer but . . . Her hair!

As Mrs Dunmore began her start-of-term lecture about the importance of hard work and the need for Team Spirit, Ellie began hatching her plan. For as long as Lisa was besotted with Jason, there was little chance of avoiding a meeting. But if she was really clever, maybe she could avoid him recognising her. Maybe.

* * *

71

Ellie let herself in the front door, flung her jacket over the coatstand and galloped upstairs. Her mum wouldn't be home for another half-hour; she usually fetched Becky from school on her way from the office because Becky hated everyone looking at her as she coped with the school bus.

Ellie pulled open the drawer of her bedside table and grabbed her wallet. Oh terrific! Three pounds, fifty pence – that wouldn't begin to pay for a haircut. She flung the wallet on the bed and glared at her reflection in the dressing-table mirror. If she could have her shoulder length hair cropped really short, she would be sure to look totally different – but haircuts cost loads and her allowance wasn't due for another two weeks. There was nothing for it – somehow she would have to persuade her mum to cough up the money. And that would take some doing.

She slumped down in front of her computer and logged on. The first day of term and already she had a mountain of impossible homework. Normally she would have gone over to Lisa's house and cadged some help but that was out of the question now. She would just have to tackle her history essay and that awful German translation on her own.

She pulled her German textbook from her bag.

Melissa knallte die Wohnzimmertur zu und stampfte den zugigen Flur entland zur küche.

What on earth was that supposed to mean? *Küche* – was that kitchen or cake? And *Flur*? Flower? Floor? Stupid language – what had possessed her to study it in the first place? She only took German because her dad – her real dad – had left them to go to live in Munich and she'd imagined that one day

72

she'd fly out and find him and . . .

Pull yourself together, she instructed herself firmly. That was just the daydream of a stupid kid. Get on with your work.

It was while she was flicking through her German dictionary to find the meaning of *stampfte* that her computer bleeped loudly. Marc! She flung the dictionary on to the floor and clicked into her Inbox.

```
. . . perhaps you're the only one who can
understand what it feels like if things go
wrong.
```

Not Marc. Freddie. But instead of the usual surge of disappointment mixed with irritation, Ellie felt excited. Not that she expected Freddie's e-mail to be riveting; more that she had just realised that, if she played her cards right, she need never sweat over a German translation again. All she had to do was e-mail it to Freddie and wait for the translation to wing its way back to her machine. Brilliant!

Of course, first of all she had to persuade Freddie that it was a good idea. She didn't appear to be overflowing with the milk of human kindness – maybe if Ellie talked a lot about this horse of hers, and didn't mention Marc . . .

```
Lisa told us about the accident of this little
sister of yours.
```

An involuntary shudder shimmered down Ellie's spine. Trust Lisa not to keep her mouth shut – not, of course, that she knew the full facts. Just that Becky had had an accident which had left her in a wheelchair and that they had moved to Nambridge so that she wouldn't have to keep going back to the road where it happened. No mention of Ellie's part in the whole business, no mention of what Dad had been doing – just the bare facts. So Freddie couldn't know much, Ellie thought, her eyes scanning down the screen.

```
. . . dreadfully unhappy because my father is
not the hero I always thought him to be.
Instead he has done something absolutely
terrible and I don't even know if I love him
any more.
```

Ellie wasn't sure how long she stared at the screen and it wasn't until she tried to read the paragraph again, and found the letters all blurred and misty, that she realised her eyes were filled with tears. She knew that feeling – but she had never thought anyone else would understand it. She hadn't been sure of her feelings for her dad – her stepdad, rather – for ages; on days when he was in a good mood she was sure she did love him and then, when the black moods overtook him, and he shouted and swore and stormed out of the house, leaving her mum emotionally bruised and in tears, she positively hated him. Not just for upsetting the family but for the lies. The lies that only she knew about.

And here was Freddie saying that her dad had done something awful. Something so bad that even thinking about her magical times with Marc didn't help. Ellie understood that too – last night in bed she had tried to relive those romantic evenings by the lake, but all the time the face of Jason Hill pushed all images of Marc out of her mind. Poor Freddie – what could have happened?

She pushed her homework to one side and seized the mouse. She clicked on to Compose Message and began to type.

Dear Freddie,
What has happened? What has your dad done? Is it something to do with your horse - has he said it has to be put down? Is he refusing to pay for medical treatment for it? Or is it worse than that? You can tell me because I do understand - I don't much like my dad. Well, he's not my real dad; he married my mum when I was three years old and then the next year they had Becky, my sister. He always liked her best, even before her accident. Since then - well, anyway, I do understand.

She paused. She didn't know what else to say; if Freddie wanted to tell her more, she would. So now she had better just carry on with a normal sort of chatty message.

I guess we have to face the fact that Marc was seeing both of us. I can't believe it and I don't want to believe it; he was so loving, so romantic to me, and you mustn't forget that his

75

letters keep talking about wanting to see me again. Has he asked to see you again? I don't think so. I also don't think being called a witch is very romantic at all – mind you, cabbages aren't exactly hot stuff, are they?!! I guess the French language isn't up to much.

I don't want to add to your problems but I guess the fact that he slipped an English sentence into his letter is a kind of clue to which one of us he is really keen on. I read in this psychology book that your subconscious mind works even when you are trying to pretend to be something you are not. Maybe Marc is trying to be really sweet to you when all the time he is fighting his passion for me. You could ask him – my languages aren't up to complicated things like that.

Talking of languages, can I ask you a favour? Each week I get German translation homework and I'm awful at it. But I want to get better because – well anyway, I have my reasons. If I e-mail it to you, would you translate it for me? I know it's a bit of a cheek to ask but maybe I could do something for you. My Maths is quite good, if that helps. Let me know what you think – and in the meantime, what does *"Melissa knallte die Wohnzimmertür zu und stampfte den zugigen Flur entlang zur küche"* mean?

```
Cheer up - whatever your dad has done, he is
still your dad, which is more than I can say
about mine. My real dad went to Germany, by
the way. Which is kind of why I want to get
better at German. For what it's worth.
Write soon,
Love Ellie
```

Ellie was just beginning to wonder if this whole e-mail wasn't just a bit over the top when the front door slammed. Mum!

She jumped up, fixed a loving, daughterly smile on her face and sped downstairs, ready to offer to fix supper, help Becky with her piano practice, wash the floor – anything, in fact, in exchange for a new hairdo.

As she rounded the bend in the stairs, she stopped dead, her mouth dropping open.

"Hello, Ellie," said her stepfather. "I'm home."

@ @ @

Rieke sat at her desk and tried to concentrate on the Maths problems in front of her. But her thoughts kept returning to her worries and her shoulders sagged a little, while she pondered over the missing period, the missing message from Marc, the missing money in the family purse and the missing father, who gambled the family's security away. Surely if

Mammi didn't find a way out they would have to move to a drab little apartment in Bremen city, Merlin would have to be sold, the boys would never come to visit them again as there wouldn't be any room for more than Mammi, Basti and her . . .

Stop! she told herself. You're getting melodramatic. She sighed, closed her book and tapped on the keys of the keyboard to her left.

She had known it – still no message from Marc. She had asked him quite openly if he had something going on with Ellie, but he had not yet answered.

What if Ellie was right? If he really had been cheating on her? Or, come to that, cheating on them both?

Impossible! Absolutely impossible! Her heart lurched and ached, and she felt the tears grating behind the lids.

No! This would not do! She opened her Maths book again, when suddenly a new message appeared on the screen. She fumbled with the keys and read:

    . . . I can't believe it and I don't want to
believe it . . .

Exactly her thoughts! Coming from a girl she really couldn't stand, she didn't like at all!

I don't want to add to your problems . . .

Who are you kidding, Ellie? You have done nothing else so far but adding problems . . .

. . . he is fighting his passion for me . . .

Oh, come on now! What a laugh! Passion for Ellie Finch? If Rieke had not felt so miserable, she would have laughed! But then she squinted her eyes. What was that?

. . . can I ask you a favour? . . . I know it
is a bit of a cheek . . .

Absolutely true it is, Miss Finch! You really flatter yourself you could help me with my Maths? This must be a joke!

Cheer up - whatever your dad has done, he is
still your dad, which is more than . . .

Hey, that sounded different, somehow quite friendly . . .

Rieke was interrupted in her musings by a soft knock at her door. "Come in," she said, wondering what Basti could have brought up to her room. "I won't trade vacuuming the sitting-room for cleaning the kitchen, if this is what you came for," she said.

"Eh, this is not what I've come about," said Paps' voice behind her.

She turned around and stared at her father. "Oh, Paps, come in. I thought it was Basti."

Her father entered her room and shut the door behind him. His eyes wandered around the walls but did not meet hers. She looked at his pale face and realised that he had not shaved – and it was already five o'clock in the afternoon!

"Yes, Paps? What is it?"

He still did not look at her, but out of the window. He cleared his voice. "Well, I just wanted to ask you . . ." His voice trailed off.

"What?"

"Oh, nothing much really. You know, I mislaid my wallet and I have to buy some things and I thought . . ."

"Yes?" Her heart felt like a cold stone. This could not happen! This was not real! This was worse than every nightmare she had had so far!

"Well, I need about a hundred marks and I thought you could . . ." Again his gaze wandered around the room, finally fixing itself on her computer.

"You want me to lend you money? A hundred marks?"

"Well – yes . . . eh . . ."

"Paps, look at me, please, just for a moment."

His eyes met hers, but only for an instant, then he looked down to the floor.

"Paps, Mammi told us about your gambling. Even if I had the money, which I don't, I would not . . ."

"But you don't understand!" His voice sounded tortured and his face showed agony. "None of you understands! I have a terrific, foolproof system; it only needs another trial run and then we'll be rich and . . ." He coughed. His pallor had given way to a feverish red glow in his face, while he tried to find the right words.

"Paps, you should talk to Mammi. She said she would try to help you if you . . ."

"Help? I don't need help! I need a little bit of money to

complete my system, that's all! I thought I could rely on you, I thought you of all my children . . ." He looked at her pleadingly.

"Don't, Paps. Don't talk like this. We talked about your system, all of us, all the boys were here and we all agreed that none of us wanted to be millionaires, that we were fine as we were before you had this get-rich-quick scheme . . ."

"It is no scheme!" her father shouted. "Talking about a scheme! It is an absolutely foolproof system, mathematically proven. It will work, I'm sure, I only need a little sum for going through the last trial run," he repeated and coughed again.

Rieke was crying silently now. The tears were streaming over her cheeks. It was exactly as Mammi had explained. She had prophesied that Paps would stop short of nothing in trying to get money, and he was.

"Sorry, Paps, I'm so sorry," she sobbed, "but it is no question of wanting to or not – I just don't have that much money. I have to save to help pay the vet, you know!"

"Stupid horse," her father whispered, while turning and leaving her room. "Stupid damn horse!"

When the door closed behind her father, Rieke threw her arms on the table and cried her heart out. How could it be that Paps, her adored Paps, had changed so terribly? Since her return from France she had seen him only when they passed each other while one was leaving and the other was entering the house, or when he came into the kitchen to grab a bite. But he had always been a quiet person, so his reticence was nothing alarming – it seemed only a bit more noticeable than usual. Until the evening of the family conference she had had absolutely no idea of how badly he had changed! Even when her mother had explained about his addiction, a tiny fraction of Rieke's heart had still insisted that Mammi was wrong, that everything was a terrible misunderstanding . . . but now she knew it was not. The Paps today was a stranger to her, and realising this made her cry even harder.

Afterwards she went to the bathroom and blew her nose and examined her panty-liner – in what had become a nearly hourly routine.

Still nothing.

Well then. Damn.

Rieke returned to her desk and opened the Maths book. But the screen was still on, Ellie's message plain and clear. And Rieke started typing.

Ach, Ellie, it is more terrible than I thought! No, it is nothing with my horse; Merlin is recovering very nicely. The thing is – well, I almost don't know how to say it in German and it is even more difficult in English. The thing is, my Paps is gambling. There you are. Now I've said it. He has changed terribly since I came back from France. I have seen him only a few times and he has changed into another person.

Can you imagine that he was here half an hour ago and tried to borrow money from me? He has a "terrific system, absolutely sure to win him millions" and he is away most of the time to lose all our family's money at some roulette table or whatever he favours for trying out his stupid system. My mother said it has something to do with him being one of those computer wizards, that the idea of a perfect mathematical system sometimes goes to their heads and makes them believe weird things.

So now you know.

Nobody else knows. I don't dare tell even my best friends about it, not even Anna. I sit in school and my classmates seem like aliens who have no idea at all what life is all about. This is not laughter and silly jokes, it is naked, plain fright. At least so it seems to me. If you want you can joke about it or humiliate me – I don't care any more.

I am afraid I am pregnant, I have a father who is a gambling junkie and I don't know if we can afford Merlin much longer. Somehow my world is upside-down and I doubt if Marc could put it right even if he wanted to, which I have come to doubt. I am terribly tired and unhappy and I wonder why I have written to you all this stuff.

Perhaps so that you can hurt me where it hurts most, what do you think?

Freddie

PS The translation for your sentence is something like: Melissa shut the sitting-room door with a loud bang and marched along the draughty hall to the kitchen.

PPS I could do with a little help right now with my Maths, as my thoughts keep wandering and I find it hard to concentrate on figures. I'll send them as an attachment and we'll see if you can help me.

@ @ @

"I'm going upstairs to do my homework!" Ellie pushed back her chair, scrunching up her table napkin and hurling it on to the table.

"But, Ellie – we haven't had dessert yet!" protested her mother. She turned to Ellie's stepdad. "If only I had known you would be back, darling, I would have made you that chocolate mousse you love, but . . ."

"I'm not hungry!" interjected Ellie.

"Are you sick?" Her mother was immediately anxious.

Yes! Ellie wanted to shout. Sick of the way you simper and fawn over that man, sick of the way you never assert yourself, sick of the way he uses you, sick of it all!

"I'm fine," she said with a weak smile. "We've just been given loads of homework, and I want to get on with it."

Her stepdad leaned back in his chair, patted his ample stomach and raised an eyebrow. "Well now," he said sarcastically, "this is an event! Ellie Finch doing some work for a change! I can't see that lasting very long."

Ellie's mum looked nervous and chewed her lip. "She's going

84

to try really hard this term, Dave," she said, with a pleading note in her voice. "She knows how important it is, don't you, Ellie?"

"Yes!" Ellie spat the word out and stormed upstairs, letting the dining-room door slam behind her. Furiously she tried to hold back the tears. She wouldn't let that man get to her, she wouldn't! He tried to pretend that she was lazy, but she wasn't. She did try hard – it wasn't her fault that she wasn't as clever as Becky.

Why did he have to come back? she thought, crashing through her bedroom door. And then immediately felt guilty. Her mum's face had lit up when she had come in from work to find Dad standing in the kitchen, brewing a pot of tea. Becky had burst into tears of joy as he had swung her up in the air and smothered her cheek with kisses. He had been really chatty to start with, telling them that the break, as he called it, had given him the chance to clear his head and that now, things would be just great.

"What's more, I've landed a new job!" he had announced, producing a bottle of sparkling wine from a carrier bag. "So let's celebrate!"

Her mum had gasped. "A new job?" she had asked. "That's wonderful! Where? What?"

Her dad had prised the cork from the bottle. "Head of maintenance," he said proudly. "In charge of all the upkeep and supplies and repairs at Nambridge College."

And while her mum had exclaimed in delight and Becky had told her dad he was brill and ace, Ellie had stared out of the window and tried very hard not to feel sick.

The college. Where Jason Hill was a student. And where

her stepdad would be working every day of his life.

And if her dad and Jason came face to face – and they would be sure to come face to face some time, wouldn't they? – then anything could happen.

And none of it bore thinking about.

Except, she thought now as she slumped down in front of her computer, she couldn't stop thinking about it, or about all the things that had happened that day four years ago. Would Jason remember it all too? Well, obviously he would remember the accident – but would he recall what led up to it? Would he remember faces? Or would it all be a blur, something he had blotted out of his memory and forgotten?

"You must try to put it all behind you!" That's what everyone had said in the weeks and months following the accident. And she had tried. But she couldn't. Not completely. Maybe it was that way for Jason too. Not that he deserved to forget.

But she did very much hope that he had.

Reluctantly she pulled her homework diary from her bag and flicked through the pages to find her new assignments. Geography: compare and contrast the geological strata of . . . No way. Science: an essay about photosynthesis. You've got to be joking! History: a day in the life of a London family in the Blitz. She'd try that – the Internet was bound to have a website on the Second World War – she could pinch bits from that.

She logged on to her computer but before she could even locate the search engine, the machine bleeped loudly: New Message!

As she went into Outlook Express, a message sprang on to the screen.

"You have an unsent message in your Outbox – do you want to send it now?"

"Oh yes!" Ellie said impatiently, clicking the appropriate box. "I mean – no!! No!" But it was too late. The sexy message that Lisa had typed – the one Ellie had meant to tone down a bit – was already winging its way to France.

This just wasn't her day.

She clicked the Inbox icon and sighed. As she had guessed – Freddie again! Please don't let it be to say that she has heard from Marc – please!

```
. . . more terrible than I thought . . . my
Paps is gambling.
```

Ellie gasped and leaned closer to the screen, her eyes scanning the tightly typed words. Poor Freddie! To have a father who'd do something like that! Even her stepdad wouldn't sink that low.

```
. . . nobody else knows. I don't dare tell even
my best friends . . .
```

Ellie felt a wave of sympathy. She knew only too well what it was like to live with a secret you could never share, to spend nights and days churning the thoughts over and over in your mind, until you thought you might go mad. No way would she joke about it, whatever Freddie might think.

"What?" Ellie was so astonished by the next paragraph that she shouted out loud. Pregnant? Freddie? What in the name of . . . ?

But there was no more. No explanation of this extraordinary statement, just something about the horse and how tired she was.

And a postscript with the translation of Ellie's homework. Even in the middle of all this stress, Freddie had actually bothered to help her out. Maybe she wasn't so bad after all. Maybe her stuck-up attitude and the way she wanted to hog the limelight was just a way of covering up her own muddles and insecurities.

But hang on! Freddie thought she was pregnant. And you only get pregnant one way. And who was it that she had been boasting about loving and hanging out with and cuddling and . . .

No!

It couldn't . . . she couldn't . . .

She could.

She might have.

But surely, she had too much sense?

But if Freddie really was pregnant, then there was one obvious candidate for who was responsible.

Marc.

Her Marc.

But if Freddie was pregnant, then Marc wasn't hers at all.

Dear Freddie,
I don't know where to start. Well, actually I do.
Let's get one thing clear: I am not going to
laugh at you, or joke about your situation or
tease you about your father's gambling. You may
think I am the pits but I don't sink that low.

88

It's awful about your father and his gambling
- and the worst bit is that he asked you for
money. Nothing makes me angrier than when
parents drag you into the messes they have made
of their lives and then expect you to help
bale them out. My dad - no, I'm fed up with
referring to him as my dad - my STEPDAD is
just the same. When Becky had her accident, he
was . . .

Ellie stopped and deleted that last half-sentence. What was
she thinking of? No way could she tell Freddie the truth; no
one knew the whole story. No one except her and Jason Hill.
And her stepfather.

Anyway, what is going to happen? Will your dad
go to one of those Gamblers Anonymous places? Do
you have them in Germany? My stepdad went to
Alcoholics Anonymous for a while; he's meant to
go still but I guess he skives off. Will you
have to move house? That's the worst part of
things going wrong - selling up and starting
over in some new place where you don't know
anyone.

She paused, her fingers hovering over the keyboard. It was
dead important that she got this next bit right. If she didn't,
Freddie would clam up and then she'd never find out anything.

You said you thought you might be pregnant. Are you sure? I mean - do you have a boyfriend back in Germany? Or did you and Marc - well, you know. Get it together? I guess you didn't - I mean even you are not that daft, surely? I can't imagine what you must be feeling like - are you being sick? My mum was sick as anything when she was expecting Becky. Mind you, Becky is enough to make anyone sick. I shouldn't say that - I mean, not after all she has been through. It's just that everyone makes such a fuss of her and she plays up to it, and I feel like a spare part in my own family. Sometimes I wish I knew where my own real dad was so that I could whizz off in the school holidays and spend time with him. Loads of my mates have parents who are divorced and they get two holidays and two Christmases and everything - and I'm stuck with a stepdad who hates my guts and a sister who makes me feel guilty every time I look at her.

I guess I shouldn't have written all that but I reckon that we are getting past the holding back secrets stage, don't you? I mean, I know you are worried about being pregnant (maybe) and about your dad and everything - so I don't suppose it much matters that you know stuff about me. The thing is, there is this guy called Jason Hill who was the cause of everything that happened to my sister - well,

partly the cause but the rest is too awful to
write about. Anyway, he's moved to Nambridge.
And worse – my best friend Lisa (the one who
played the sax at camp) is going out with him.
It's like a nightmare and there's no escape.
You see, I'm bound to have to meet him soon,
because Lisa is so crazy about him that she
wants to show him off to everyone – and when
Jason sees me, he will recognise me. He always
said he'd get me one day and I'm scared.

  Anyway, I going to get all my hair cut off –
assuming I can get my mum to cough up the
money. Do you think I'll look really different
with cropped hair? I've got to look different.
By Wednesday.
Love Ellie

PS Have you tried a hot bath? Or skipping really
fast with a skipping rope? That's supposed to
make overdue periods come. Good luck.
PPS Have you heard from Marc? Have you told him
that you think you're pregnant? Or was it
another boyfriend? If it was, you were two-
timing him as well, weren't you?
PPPS Good luck. Really. I mean it.
PPPPS Thanks for the translation. I had a go at
your Maths – I hope it helps!

When Rieke woke up two hours before her usual time she waited for a few moments, scared that she would feel that terrible sickness again.

Nothing. She felt all right. Absolutely all right. With a jump she got out of bed and headed for the bathroom. Great! It had all been her imagination. Everything was going to be all right.

It happened while she was brushing her teeth. Without the slightest warning, the sudden cramp in her stomach made her vomit right into the basin. When the urge ended, her knees were trembling and she sat down on the rim of the bathtub. Nothing was all right.

She waited until the shivering had stopped and her heartbeats were back to normal, then she showered and went back to her room. While dressing, she checked if there was a message from Marc – no.

She felt let down. How could he let her down when she was feeling so terrible – even if he knew nothing about it. He should have cared.

There was no message from Ellie Finch either. So what? Rieke didn't know why she even bothered to think about it. That girl was full of malice, lies, insinuations . . . And even worse – she was the only one who knew the truth about Rieke's fears and that disgraceful thing with Paps!

Rieke gritted her teeth and clicked off-line.

When Rieke walked downstairs, her mother called from the study: "Is that you, Rieke? Could you please come here for a moment?"

When Rieke entered the study, she found her mother

already sitting behind the huge desk belonging to her father, sorting some papers.

"I want to tell you some important things."

Rieke looked down at her. Mammi somehow looked smaller than she had before the holidays, and the fine lines around her eyes had deepened. The wrinkles on her forehead were more visible.

"I had a meeting with the lawyer and spoke to a colleague of mine at the university, who is a specialist in the field of the psychology of addictions. First, I have taken my name off the joint bank account and I have opened my own separate account where your father can't touch my salary.

"Second: he will try to get money from everybody, and I'm afraid he won't stop short of you."

Rieke swallowed hard. Her mother's eyes widened. "What – no! He . . . ?"

Rieke nodded. "Yes – he wanted a hundred marks for an absolutely perfect winning system. But I told him I had no money to give him."

Her mother had put her hands before her face. Now she let them drop. She looked terribly tired.

"Oh no. How could he sink so low? But it's exactly what I was told to expect. Well," the ghost of a smile flickered over her face, "at least he did not succeed. As you've probably realised, I've put away all our valuable things, so that he can't take them to the pawn shop or sell them."

Only then Rieke saw that the silver candlesticks which usually stood on the windowsill had disappeared, as had the silver photo frames from the bookcase.

Her mother had followed her gaze. "Yes, that, and I've put the silverware in the safe, too, and other things." She sighed. "It is terrible that we have to treat him like a child – but people with addictions aren't responsible for their actions any more. At least, not fully."

Rieke went round the desk, put her arms round her mother and gave her a kiss. "I'm so sorry for you! It's you who've been hit the worst by all this. And you have done nothing to deserve it."

Her mother smiled again, but it was a sad smile. "I'm not too sure about that. If I had not been so occupied with my research and if I hadn't accepted that post at the university in New York I might have seen this coming and perhaps I could have prevented it. He was often alone during those years we were abroad and this obviously has led him to the casinos."

She paused, brushing a stray strand of hair from her eyes. "Anyway," she added briskly, "I am willing to face my responsibility if only I can get him to go to therapy with me. But – we'll see. Perhaps in time I can persuade him."

But she didn't sound too hopeful.

Rieke went back upstairs to her room and sat on her bed, staring at the wall. This was really the worst moment to add to her mother's problems her own fear of being pregnant.

Should she tell Marc?

How many times had she pondered over this? But how could he help? Would he react like so many boys and men in the novels she had read: disbelieving, put out, outraged, even infuriated?

Rieke's heart ached for one of those beautiful things he'd whispered in her ears when they were together during those unforgettable sweet hours in the little shed. The shed which Ellie also knew.

She switched on her computer and checked again. A message from Ellie. Rieke grimaced at the screen, but she clicked the icon to get it from the Inbox.

Her eyes widened as she scanned the lines of type and came to rest at the end.

Two-timing? Her! Having another boyfriend!

That was thick, even coming from Ellie Finch! How dare she! That girl had such a repulsive imagination! Asking if she and Marc . . .

Well, but wasn't this the question which was haunting her too?

What had happened that night when she had fallen asleep because of too much sun, too much swimming, too much playing volleyball during the day. Had he . . . ?

But wouldn't she have woken up? Of course she would.

But why had she been sick again this morning? Hadn't she once read that story *The Marquise of O*, where a woman had been raped while unconscious?

Stop it! she told her vivid imagination. Stop it! This is not literature from an author named Kleist, this is real life in the twentieth century – such things don't happen!

Do they?

But in the message from Ellie there were also some quite different feelings: sympathy, understanding, even consolation.

95

Rieke read it again and sat there wondering. Ellie was asking for her help. Ellie had a bag of problems herself — that was evident. There was something about her sister's accident that sounded quite mysterious . . .

And what was that about Gamblers Anonymous?

And what did she mean by getting past the holding back secrets stage? They had not been holding back, had they?

Was Ellie talking about being honest? Hadn't Rieke been honest with Ellie Finch? Well, why not? She had nobody else she could be honest with, had she?

To: Ellie Finch <elliefin@email.com>
From: Friederike Hofmann <ahofmann@uni-bremen.de>
Date: Tue, 5 Sept 2000 07:45:22
Subject: **Hairy**

Dear Ellie,
Thank you for your sympathy. Actually I was
surprised. I had been afraid you would be
jeering. Obviously you are not quite the Ellie I
thought I knew. As for another boyfriend —
sorry, my one and only love was and is Marc.
And my fears still exist. But thanks for your
suggestions — if nothing happens today I will
try everything to make that cursed period come.

I honestly don't understand why that Jason
Hill person is making you so frightened — were
you in love with him once? Has he rejected
you? Are you jealous of Lisa? (Of course I

know who played the sax so penetratingly and tinnily!!!) What does this mean, "he will get you"? Is he after you because of your oh-so-sweet personality? Or is he threatening you?

But if you really do want to change your look, I'd suggest not only a new haircut, but a different colour as well. As my brother Basti has often experimented with hair dying during the last years, I happen to know quite a lot about it. You can choose a 'natural' colour: in your case blonde, red or black - anything except brown. But I think the disguising effect would be much stronger if you used one of those crazy blues, violets, oranges or greens. For this you need only food dyes - you know, those little tubes you can buy in food shops, which the bakers use to colour marzipan. But with blue, green and violet there is a little problem: you have to bleach your hair first, otherwise the colour wouldn't be noticeable.

But in any case, you should probably inform your parents first or it might lead to a heart attack, when you suddenly enter the room glorying in an orange crew cut. And on the other hand, if hair dying is not *en vogue* in your school right now you'd be quite conspicuous and you might draw extra attention to yourself when you'd rather not. If you don't get those mega-hip colours in your town, write

to me and I'll send them to you WITH
translated instructions.

By the way - if this Jason person is really
bothering you, you could always look up your
dad in Munich and on your way down the country
you could visit me - if you don't mind
gambling-addicted fathers, absent-minded,
terribly preoccupied mothers and absent
brothers.

Anyway, I send you also my love and hope
that you solve all your little problems.
(Sending love sounds strange, doesn't it? Do
you think we could get used to it?)
Freddie

PS Your suggestions made me think of something!!
Tomorrow I'll get a pregnancy test in a
pharmacy! Then I'll know!
PPS Why, oh why, didn't I think of that before?
PPPS Perhaps I am much too frightened to get
the wrong answer.
PPPPS I haven't thanked you yet for those
equations - they helped me quite a lot. Fancy
that algebra is an international language, huh?

Rieke sent the message and checked her Inbox. Another
message!

This time it was the longed-for, the long-awaited:

Ma petite sorcière,

J'ai peu de temps – je dois aller travailler en deux secondes – mais je devrait te dire que je t'aime encore plus qu'avant . . .

Ricke read on and devoured every word. So he still loved her and thought about her! How could she ever have doubted him? That was all Ellie's fault. If she hadn't lied about having been Marc's girlfriend too . . .

But somehow the happiness was not the same overwhelming feeling she had known before. Somehow his words lacked something . . .

She read again and tried to pinpoint what had made her so uneasy, when Basti poked his head round her door. "Come on, Mammi has said she'll drop us at school on her way in – but we need to leave now."

Sighing, Rieke shut down her computer and picked up her bag. She was not looking forward to this!

School was strange. Rieke sat there during the lessons, gave answers and asked questions and had the feeling she was watching herself from another planet. Surely this girl did nothing to make other people guess that something was not as it should be. Something? Everything, more like.

During break she even managed a nearly normal conversation with Anna. It was only when Anna gave her the time when she was to come over after school that Rieke realised that she had agreed to meet her. "Sorry," she mumbled, "I just forgot about a promise I made. I have to help my mother this afternoon. And I want to check on Merlin. Another time, OK?"

Anna looked at her resignedly. "I don't know what's happened to you since France. Falling in love with French boys can't be such a wonderful thing after all. This Marc has made a recluse out of you."

Rieke laughed. "Oh no, it's only the cold northern climate that's got to me, that's all." But even to her own ears it sounded unconvincing.

Anna gave her another doubtful look and turned away to talk to another girl.

At the end of the day Rieke sped out of school and hurried home before anyone could catch her. Thankfully no one was home yet. She went up to her room and lay on her bed, holding Fritz. She just wanted a couple of hours of peace and quiet, without any more hassles . . .

Suddenly a door slammed downstairs, footsteps pounded on the stairs and Basti shouted, "Rieke! Rieke! Come down! Fast! Paps has taken Merlin away! Mammi is afraid he is trying to sell him!"

To: Friederike Hofmann <ahofmann@uni-bremen.de>
From: Ellie Finch <elliefin@email.com>
Date: Tue, 5 Sept 2000 08:56:48
Subject: **Brainwave!**

Dear Freddie,

Thanks for the advice - that's a great idea!
I'm going auburn - I've bought some hair colour
from the chemist round the corner and it says
it's dead easy to do. I can't go violet - you
get expelled for things like that at Nambridge
High; stuffy or what? And as for warning the
parents: forget it! My mum is still swooning all
over my stepdad because he's finally come home -
I didn't tell you about that, did I? He is for
ever storming off for days on end and then coming
back as if nothing had happened. Anyway, there
is one good thing about Mum's new-found state of
bliss - I asked her for the money for a haircut
and she handed it over without a murmur! "Just
a little trim, darling," she said. As if! I
know she will go ballistic when she sees it,
but by then it will be too late, won't it? And
as for my stepdad, he is always finding fault
with me, so I might as well give him something
positive to yell about. Anyway, after school
this afternoon I'm off to the hairdressers and
then tonight, I'm going to dye what's left. I'm
even thinking of tinting my eyebrows - cool, eh?

    I don't have time to explain about Jason
right now - but NO WAY was I in love with him!
I didn't even like the jerk.

That's a lie, Ellie thought, her fingers pausing in their frantic
typing. After all, if you hadn't liked him, you wouldn't have . . .
Stop. Stop right now.

Just thinking about it makes me feel sick.
Anyway, I've got to dash now - I'll let you
know how the hair goes. Good luck at the
pharmacy.
Love Ellie

PS It's German today so we'll see how your
translation stands up.

Ellie clicked on the Send icon and was about to switch off the
computer when the words New Message! flashed on the screen.
    Marc! It had to be Marc.
    It was.
    Ellie's heart beat faster as she glanced impatiently at her
watch. If she waited to read his message, she would be late for
meeting Lisa. But she had to read it; she had to know.
    She pored over the French, trying to get the meaning from
the words she recognised.

My little cabbage . . . I am in a hurry . . . I
have to be at work in a couple of seconds . . .

tell you how much I love you - even more than I
loved before, I think. I am in much hurrying.
Ich liebe dich, meine Friederike.
Marc

Ellie sat motionless, tears springing to her eyes. Her heart,
which had soared as she began to read the message, began
pounding in her ears.

Ich liebe dich, meine Friederike.

He thought he was writing to that girl. To Friederike. So it
was true. She couldn't deny it any longer. Marc was two-timing
her.

She would kill Freddie. And to think that she'd been on the
point of confiding her innermost thoughts and feelings to that
two-timing, double-crossing, immoral, unprincipled little . . .

"Ellie! Hurry up! You're going to be late!" Her mother's
voice wafted up the stairs.

Ellie swallowed hard and zapped the computer. Just you
wait, Miss Friederike Hofmann, she thought, snatching up her
schoolbag and stomping down the stairs. She stormed
through the hall and out of the front door, ignoring her
mother's shouted farewell. She couldn't speak to anyone
because if she did, she knew she would burst into tears.

She couldn't face meeting Lisa – but then, she couldn't face
her friend's reaction if she didn't turn up. Reluctantly she
turned the corner and headed for the crossroads where they
always met.

The knot in the pit of her stomach tightened as she
remembered those wonderful weeks in France. Marc, how

could you? What about all those times you told me you loved me, said that I was the sweetest girl you had ever met, that no one had ever made you feel the way I did? What about those evenings in the shed, when you stroked my hair and kissed my lips? What about the romantic e-mail you sent me just a couple of days ago, the one Lisa had translated and . . .

The thought hit her with such force that she stopped dead in the middle of the pavement.

Lisa's reply – the one that talked about lips and breasts and being his for ever – would have reached him by now. She could just imagine it! He'd be laughing, showing it to all his mates, jeering at the English kid who thought she was his one and only love. And he would probably write to Freddie, and they'd laugh about the way they had conned her and say what a total jerk she was.

Because now it was all abundantly clear. Freddie and Marc really had been an item. She should have seen it – after all, Freddie wouldn't be worrying herself sick about being pregnant if she didn't have good cause. So all the time that Marc had been murmuring sweet nothings into Ellie's ear, he had been planning his next meeting with Freddie.

"Hi, Ellie! Over here!"

Ellie was jolted out of her reverie by a familiar voice. Lisa was standing on the other side of the road, waving frantically.

Automatically, Ellie started to cross the road.

And stopped.

Leaning against a lamp post beside Lisa was a tall guy with bleached blond hair curling over the collar of his leather jacket. He was twirling a strand of Lisa's hair between his fingers and nibbling the back of her neck.

Jason Hill. It had to be Jason.

Ellie turned and belted along the street, round the corner and into the newsagent. He hadn't seen her; he had been too taken up with Lisa. Ellie's heart was pounding loudly as she grabbed a magazine from the shelf and buried her head in it, her eyes constantly darting towards the doorway.

Seeing Jason had brought it all back. He'd been flirting like that the day it happened and Ellie, even at the age of ten and a half, had been madly jealous of Verity, the girl he was with. She was only thirteen, but dead cool and Ellie had wanted so much to be like her. After all, she was going out with a fifteen-year-old and that just proved how sophisticated she was. If only, Ellie had thought, she could look like Verity and talk like Verity, someone like Jason would fall madly in love with her and she would be happy for ever.

As if, thought Ellie now, flicking unseeingly through the pages of the magazine and praying that Lisa and Jason would give up waiting for her. What a dumb kid I was! I used to follow Jason and Verity everywhere – more fool me! If only I'd stayed away, if only I hadn't gone down to the park that evening . . .

The bell on the shop door tinkled and Ellie jumped out of her skin. But it was only a harassed mother dragging a couple of toddlers behind her.

Ellie looked at her watch. She'd have to go – she was going to be late for registration as it was.

Please God, she breathed, don't let them see me. Not yet. Not till after tonight. Please.

* * *

"So what was it with you?" demanded Lisa as they filed into their German lesson. "And don't say you didn't see me, because I know you did."

Ellie took a deep breath and launched into the excuse she had been so carefully practising. "Actually," she said, deliberately lowering her voice and leaning towards Lisa, "it was my period. I was standing there, waiting to cross and then – zap! Just like that! Three days early, can you believe? I was so embarrassed – I had to dash to the chemist to get supplies. I'm really sorry."

To her relief, Lisa nodded sympathetically. "It's awful when that happens, isn't it?" she agreed. "I was on holiday once and we were on this boat and . . ."

But Ellie wasn't listening. In the middle of telling her story and talking about periods, a terrible thought had struck her. If Freddie's period didn't come and she really was pregnant, what would happen to her? She still insisted that Marc was her one and only love – but clearly Marc didn't see it that way. He may have forgotten he was writing to Ellie and started using German phrases – but hadn't Freddie said that he'd slipped into English when he was e-mailing her? So how many more girls were getting loving e-mails? How many more girls were dreaming that Marc was theirs and theirs alone?

". . . so is that OK, then?" Lisa's insistent voice broke in on her musings.

"What?"

Lisa sighed impatiently. "If we meet at the cinema tomorrow – about eight? I need you as my alibi. There's this dead good film with Gwyneth Paltrow – and you can meet Jason."

"Well . . ." Ellie hesitated.

"Oh come on!" urged Lisa. "I need you there – as my alibi. That way, I can tell the parents I'm out with you and they won't go ballistic."

Ellie swallowed. There was no way out of it, and besides, she'd have her new hairdo by then. And cinemas were dark and nobody had to make conversation.

"Yeah, cool," she said, pulling her textbook from her schoolbag. "Can't wait."

"Skinhead, skinhead, Ellie's got a skinhead!"

"Shut up, you little toerag!"

"Don't you speak to your sister like that, young lady! She's worth ten of you and . . ."

"Oh, Dave love, don't be like that!"

More than all the shouting and name-calling, her mum's meek pleading got under Ellie's skin. Why couldn't she stand up for her properly, tell him that he had no right to talk down to her? After all, he wasn't her real dad.

"What do you think you look like?" her stepfather sneered. "A common, tarty little . . ."

"SHUT UP!" The words were out before she could stop them. She saw her mum flinch and Becky's mouth drop open as she shot an anxious glance in her dad's direction. "I can look however I like and you can't stop me!"

In an instant, he had pushed his chair back and was standing, towering over her. "How dare you speak to me like that?" he thundered. "Get up to your room now and don't come down! You make me sick."

"The feeling," retorted Ellie, biting hard on her lip, "is entirely mutual."

You mustn't cry, she told herself, shutting her bedroom door behind her. If he comes up to check on you, don't give him the satisfaction of seeing that you're upset.

Ellie slumped down in front of her dressing-table mirror. OK, so it wasn't quite what she had planned. Her shoulder-length brown hair had gone, to be replaced by a three-centimetre crop. That bit was OK – in fact, she reckoned it showed her bone structure off to good advantage.

The bit that was seriously wrong was the colour. Burnished Gold, the label had said. She had rushed home from the hairdressers and by the time her mum and Becky got back, she was swathed in a towel waiting for the colour to take. And then her mum had decided she should lay the table, and then she'd made her phone her gran and somehow the fifteen minutes that the instructions had specified had stretched to half an hour.

And she wasn't burnished gold at all. She was a horrible, brassy orange.

Her mum had cried and her sister had laughed. And then her stepdad had shouted those terrible things. Tears welled up in Ellie's eyes. How could she show her face at school in the morning? Why had she listened to Freddie Hofmann? Her and her clever ideas about hair colour. Well, maybe she could come up with some quaint German folk remedy for this mess.

Ellie crossed to her computer and switched it on.

Dear Freddie,
You have to help. The hair is a disaster – it's
bright orange and it was meant to be a
sophisticated sort of pale auburn. So what do I
do? I don't dare start on my eyebrows, so they
are still dark brown and I look totally naff.

I'm so miserable. Not just about the hair,
about everything. I might as well tell you – I
got an e-mail today from Marc, and in the
middle of it he wrote "*Ich liebe dich, meine
Friederike.*" I can just see you now, sitting
there all smug and self-satisfied. But before
you gloat too much, don't forget that in the
middle of your e-mail, he wrote in English. Get
it? It's pretty clear if you ask me – he is
definitely two-timing us. And how many other
girls is he writing to? I really thought he
loved me – I did things with him I've never
done with any other guy. Oh, not THAT – but
you know, proper kissing and cuddling and
stuff. I might as well be honest – I've never
had a proper boyfriend before. I've been out
with guys from school to the cinema or bowling
– but it's never got beyond holding hands or a

quick damp slurp on the cheek. English boys are so – immature. What are Germans like? I mean, Marc was so cool and sophisticated and I really, really thought . . .

Still, it doesn't much matter what either of us thought, does it? What are you going to do? What if you ARE pregnant? Did you do the test? Please tell me what happened. Come to think of it, I guess the outcome of that is far more important than my disastrous hair – but if you can think of anything I can do, please, please, please e-mail back as soon as you can. I'll be sitting here till bedtime – I've had a major bust-up with my stepdad over the hair epic.

Talking of dads, how's yours? Can you persuade him to go to Gamblers Anonymous? I guess you can get information off the Internet – perhaps you could leave it lying around somewhere? Sadly, there's no organisation that can turn my stepdad into a decent human being or make him come clean about what really happened . . .

Ellie stared at the screen. What was she on? She couldn't tell Freddie . . . but then again, why the hell not? Freddie was hundreds of miles away and was hardly likely to meet her dad and spill the beans. And she felt so uptight, and so alone, and so . . . scared.

. . . that evening when Becky got hurt. He's told the world it was my fault, and in some ways it was. But it was his too.

She paused again as a door slammed downstairs.

"That kid of yours drives me to drink!" she heard her stepfather shout. "Nothing but trouble, that's what she is!"

That did it. Ellie's fingers whizzed over the keyboard.

Becky liked to walk to the end of the road to meet her dad on his way home from work. Well, she was only seven, after all. Anyway, that evening Mum had told me to walk with her and said we could go as far as the corner shop and get ice creams.

Dad was ages coming and I was fed up of waiting, so I said we should go across the road to the park for a laugh. Becky said we shouldn't because we weren't allowed, but then she always was a goody-goody. Anyway, I just told her she was a drip and grabbed her hand and made her come with me.

She went on the swings and I was dead bored - so I wandered off down to this little wooded bit at the end of the park. That's where I saw him. My stepdad. I can remember it as if it was just yesterday. He was lying there under the trees on a rug with this woman. And she was - well, she had taken some of her clothes

off and they were sort of cuddling and stuff.
Like - you have to remember I was only ten.
Anyway, I must have screamed or shouted out or
something because Dad looked up and when he saw
me his face turned purple. He jumped up and
made to come after me - he was pulling on his
clothes as he came. And he gripped my shoulders
and put his face really close to mine and his
breath smelled of alcohol. And he said that if
I dared to open my mouth - well, actually he
said, "If you open your nasty little mouth and
say one word about this to anyone, I'll have
you thrown out. I don't have to keep you -
you're not my kid!"

Ellie paused to brush away the tears that were trickling down her cheek. It was crazy, she knew that; it had happened almost four years ago. But whenever she thought about it she felt small and vulnerable and scared all over again.

I think that was when the woman called out to
my stepdad. She was gesticulating wildly and he
half turned and I managed to get away. I ran,
grabbed Becky off the swings and kept running. I
ran across the grass and down to the path that
ran along the bottom of the park by the stream.
There was this gang of boys standing just along
from us - I knew some of them from school and I
didn't want them to see the state I was in, so

I ran the other way and that's when it happened.

He came from nowhere on this motorbike. Roaring along, he was, really fast. I pulled at Becky's hand but the front wheel of the bike caught her. She looked like a rag-doll being thrown into the air. The boys in the gang screamed. The guy on the bike wheeled round and kept revving the engine.

"You tell a ******** soul it was me and I'll get you!" That's what he said, Freddie. It was Jason Hill. I knew him because he went to the secondary school which was on the same site as my primary and everyone knew he was a right tearaway. But loads of us had a kind of crush on him - especially me. But suddenly he didn't seem like an idol any more - he was towering over me and his face was really hard and cruel.

"You breathe a single word and you're dead meat!" Jason yelled right close to my face and then he turned the bike back round and roared off, and the others in the gang seemed to disappear in a second. I was so scared.

After that it was all a blur. I remember seeing Becky just lying there, her leg at a weird angle with the bone sticking through the skin. I remember screaming for my dad and running towards the coppice where he'd been.

But he'd gone. Then I fainted - or at least
that's what people said afterwards.

Now the tears were streaming unchecked down Ellie's face.
Her shoulders were shaking and the taste of sour acid was in
her mouth once again. She stopped typing and buried her face
in her hands. She was ten again, sitting on the sofa with all the
grown-ups asking her questions. And all the images were
getting muddled in her head. There was her dad lying on the
grass with a strange lady and the noise of a motorbike and
Becky flying through the air. And her dad was shouting and
saying that Elinor knew she shouldn't have left the street and
her mum was crying and saying it suited her very well to
forget it all. And all Ellie had known for sure was that she
mustn't tell or someone would come and get her.

She shook herself and wiped her eyes. Enough. She had
probably said too much already.

There's a whole lot more but I have to do my
Maths now. By the way, I got A* for the German
- or rather, you did! Thanks so much - my
German teacher is in shock!!! I do hope the
test proved negative: sorry to have gone on so
much but Jason coming back is so scary because
if he does recognise me . . . but then, he
won't, will he? Not with this hair.

Write soon and tell me what we're going to
do about two-timing Marc.
Love Ellie

114

PS I'm pleased your horse is better – at least
you can gallop away from your troubles when the
mood takes you. Lucky you.

@ @ @

"Oh noooo!"

Rieke sat beside her mother in the car, howling like a little
child who had lost her most treasured toy. "He can't have
done that! He's my father! How could he?" she sobbed,
searching frantically for a tissue, because not only were her
tears streaming, her nose had started running too.

"Come on, Rieke, we'll find Merlin! Don't cry! We'll get
him back somehow!" Her mother gnawed worriedly on the
inside of her cheek, while driving as fast as she could and
trying at the same time to pat her daughter's shoulder.

But Rieke was beyond her mother's kind consolations; she
shrugged off the caressing hand and started to attack. "If only
you had paid more attention! If only you had cared more
before everything went downhill, before he . . ."

"That's enough!" snapped her mother. "If you want me to
be sorry that I confided my feelings to you, you're going the
right way about it! Now just stop behaving like a baby – and
let's start thinking what we'll do about Merlin!"

Rieke was convulsed by even more terrible sobs – now she
also felt ashamed of her tantrum.

Her mother dug into the pockets of her coat and fished out a not-too-clean hanky. "Here."

Rieke blew her nose and mumbled: "I'm sorry, I didn't know what I was saying . . ."

"Well, as long as you don't repeat any of it," her mother said, braking and bending over to kiss her cheek. "I just hope we are still in time to meet this mysterious man."

When they arrived at the Mertens' farmyard, all hell seemed to have broken loose. In the middle of the yard stood a Volvo with a horse box attached and behind this stood Farmer Mertens, holding on to Merlin's halter strap, while a man with a bald head tried to snatch the strap away from him. Both men were shouting at the top of their lungs while a little boy standing beside the car was crying, "Get it! Get it!"

When Farmer Mertens saw Mrs Hofmann he suddenly dropped the halter strap and the bald man stumbled backward and nearly fell down.

"What the hell . . . ?" he yelled, glaring at the farmer.

Rieke's mother stepped between the two men. "Could you please tell me just what you think you are doing with my daughter's horse?"

"Your daughter's . . . ?" The man's eyes nearly popped out of their sockets. "I've bought this horse from Jens Hofmann. He told me I was to come here and collect it."

"This horse does not belong to my husband, it belongs to my daughter. Would you please stop frightening the poor animal? Here, Rieke, take him back to the paddock."

Mrs Hofmann took the lead from the bald-headed man and

gave it to Rieke who led Merlin away from the yard. Usually placid and even-tempered, Merlin was shaking his head and rolling his eyes – resisting the halter strap. Gently, Rieke patted his neck and searched in her anorak pockets for a liquorice. She found a crumbling one and fed it to him, whispering soothingly to Merlin to calm down, that nobody would take him away, everything was going to be all right.

Having settled Merlin, Rieke returned to the farmyard. Her mother and the stranger were still in heated argument over the rightful ownership of the horse. But it was obvious that the stranger had no rights – and no paperwork – and cursing Jens-Jakob Hofmann, swearing that he had been cheated and would have his money back, he stormed off, with his sobbing son.

"I don't think he'll have much luck," Rieke's mother sighed as they drove home. "There is an old saying: you reach into an empty pocket, you won't find a penny. I'm only glad I separated our accounts."

But when Rieke glanced at her mother she saw a single tear rolling down her cheek. Poor Mammi, the strain had really started to show. But as for her father: HOW COULD HE?

Merlin had been her long-awaited present for her thirteenth birthday and she had cared for him as she had promised her parents, and she'd schooled him and won several rosettes with him at events during the last few years.

HOW COULD HE?!

Once home, Rieke followed her mother into the study and sat down heavily in the big leather armchair in the corner. "What can we do to stop Paps doing things like this?" she wailed.

"Well, first of all we have to get hold of him," her mother said crisply. "Go and get Basti, then we'll make a plan."

They spent the rest of the afternoon making a list of all of Paps' friends and phoning them. Nobody had seen him or talked to him for several days. They asked Anton, Felix and Johannes if they knew anything – but every time they drew a blank.

When they finally went to bed, Rieke was too exhausted to cry. She snuggled against Fritz's velvet fur and slept like a log.

When she woke up the next morning Rieke stared at the wall and tried to remember why she felt so utterly drained. Then it came back: Paps had tried to sell her horse! By a hair's-breadth they'd prevented Merlin from being taken away by a stranger!

She didn't have to be at school that day until the second lesson so she dived under her duvet, wanting to drift off to sleep again, but finally she gave up and went to the bathroom.

Still no period.

Well then, as her world was coming crashing down anyway – this might make the ultimate disaster . . .

Rieke didn't feel like eating, but automatically grabbed the buttered roll and the apple Mammi had put on the table before leaving and left to catch the bus to Bremen. But when she arrived at the bus station, she decided not to go to school, turned around and went back to the house. She sat down at the kitchen table and put her head in her hands.

To think that only two weeks ago she had been the happiest person alive, loving and feeling herself loved and everything had been pure paradise. And now?

Slowly she got up and climbed the stairs to her room, sat down at the desk and switched on her computer.

A message from Ellie!

Eagerly she punched the keys . . . there it was . . .

After she had read the first sentences she sat there and stared through the window without seeing anything. That clinched it. This was the last straw — the one that broke the camel's back — a phrase that had struck her as being so funny when she first heard it. But now it was not funny at all.

Marc was a cheat. A liar.

The most handsome boy she'd ever met in her life, the tanned, laughing, sophisticated superhero of her dreams was just a little shit, making fun of two schoolgirls by two-timing them.

Verdammte Schei'e! So ein gemeiner Mistkerl!

Rieke grimaced and read on.

Afterwards she sat there for a long time and her heart went out to that same Ellie she had fought against and hated and tried to snub.

What an odious stepfather!

That sad, weak mother!

That poor little sister!

And now — Jason Hill, of all people, who had threatened to punish her if she ever breathed a word about his part in Becky's accident.

Rieke sat there for a long time, trying to figure out how Ellie had managed for so many years to give the impression of being a tough, funny, indomitable girl . . . when she had such a truckload of problems! Then she squared her shoulders and got up. OK, moping around was no solution, feeling helpless and mistreated no excuse for doing nothing.

When she left her room Rieke heard the front door shut. Mammi and Basti had left the house before her – so who . . . ? Paps! He must have thought that nobody would be at home. Well, he was in for a little surprise.

Carefully she went down the staircase, trying very hard not to make any sound. She crept to the open kitchen door – and sure enough – there he was opening the fridge, looking for something to eat.

"Nice to see you!" She entered the kitchen.

Her father jumped and the plate with the leftovers from yesterday's dinner crashed on the tiles. "What . . . ?" He looked at her and her anger dissolved at seeing him with his stubble, dishevelled clothes and sagging shoulders. Good heavens – was this her father?

Obviously it was her day for losing all the heroes she'd ever adored.

"Why did you steal Merlin?"

"What? I – I don't understand . . ." He looked at her, bewildered.

"You sold Merlin. You had no right to do that."

She stood there in the kitchen doorway and looked at him and pitied him, but this did not make her waver in her determination.

"Sold? No, no – I only . . ." He looked at her and suddenly the tears rolled down his cheeks.

Torn with the thoughts that this was the man who used to dry her tears when she was a little girl, Rieke continued:

"What are you planning to do next? If you're going to try to sell other things we might as well be prepared."

Her father went to the kitchen table and slumped down on a chair. He put his arms on the table and laid his head on them. He went on crying silently; his shoulders heaved, but he made no sound.

Rieke felt helpless. What is one supposed to do with a weeping father? Stroke his head? Murmur consoling words? Finally she grabbed a tea towel, pushed it to him, and started to make tea.

She fetched bread and butter, wurst and cheese and laid the table. Then she poured the tea, put heaps of sugar in their cups and sat down at the opposite side of the table.

Her father had stopped crying and buttered a slice of bread.

"Why did you do this?"

He moaned. "I had gambling debts. I put Merlin up as security, but then my system – well, I never was able to really try it out. I only needed a hundred marks more, but I didn't have them . . ."

"So you gave my horse away. MY HORSE, remember? It was a present!"

"Well, I didn't want to give it away, only . . ." His voice faltered.

"Oh, yes, and now you're miserable, because all the world is ignoring your famous system." Rieke bent forwards. "You want to know something? I feel sorry for you. But I'm also furious, because you are no better than a common thief. Don't talk about systems – think about taking things which don't belong to you. Stealing from your daughter – how low can you get?"

He lifted his tearstained face. "But what can I do?"

"How should I know?" Repulsion and pity were mingled in a curious way.

He drank from his tea. "Your mother does not talk to me any more. I feel so absolutely . . ."

"What? What do you feel?"

Rieke and her father nearly jumped out of their skins at the sound of Mammi's voice. They had not heard the car or the front door opening.

Mrs Hofmann dumped her shopping bags on the clear part of the table. "Rieke, darling, we'll talk about you not being in school later. In the meantime I'd like you to go to your room, because I want to talk to your father. This is not a child's job, this is something between him and me."

Somewhat relieved, but very much worried, Rieke got up and left the room.

In the evening Rieke e-mailed Ellie.

Ellie,
You can't imagine how glad I am that you are there across the Channel to listen to me. Somehow I now think this is, after all, the best thing that's happened to me in the last weeks.

There is so much to tell and to answer that I don't know how to start.

I still can't get over your story about Becky's accident and how this has changed your life and put so much terror and fear in it. I would like so much to help you – to get you away from your stepfather and from Jason, and if you can think of a way let me know!

The other thing is Marc.

Today I went to town and into a pharmacy to get that pregnancy test. And while I was standing there waiting for my turn I suddenly experienced the most beautiful little cramp you can imagine, and right afterwards I felt a trickle down my legs and I knew: I GOT MY PERIOD! So, after all that, I didn't buy any test but sanitary towels! You can't imagine how I felt! As if a mountain had been lifted from my back! I think I must have had this thing called a hysterical pregnancy – I've had morning sickness and everything! But thankfully that's all gone now and I feel like a new woman! It's only now I've realised how much that fear of being pregnant had terrorised me all along. And not only that: I was always wondering if Marc had abused my trust and done things to me without me knowing and wanting it.

Seems that at least here he is in the clear. But I think I don't want him any more; I don't want letters other girls are getting too. I don't know how you feel about him, but I'm

through with that cheating superboy. If you're
not you can have him all bundled up in
wrapping paper. I am so happy my body belongs
to me again I think I'll stay solo for a
while.

My father is packing his old rucksack and is
going for a trek to Finland. This has come out
of a long talk he had with my mother. She told
me that when he was a young man he made these
trips every year, to clear his thoughts and to
give him time to enjoy nature, relying on his
own ability to organise his living in the
tundra. It is not really dangerous, but it
certainly is a different thing from a little
travel to a tourist area. But - and on this my
mother insisted - he will take a cellular phone
with him. I don't know if this is a therapeutic
sort of thing or if this is just a plan to give
everybody concerned breathing space. At least
there are not many Spielcasinos in Finland.

I'm glad he is going away for a little while
so I don't have to worry about Merlin all the
time I'm in school. It really gave me the most
terrible shock when we went yesterday to the
farm to find a stranger there trying to put MY
HORSE in HIS horsebox! Can you imagine? My
father had "sold" the man my horse to cover
his gambling debts. I was so furious! I thought
him a louse of a father.

I am awfully sorry about the mess with your hair. I asked in the pharmacy and they told me the best people to ask for help are hairdressers, because they have to deal with problems of that kind all the time. I know that you wear school uniforms and that sort of thing, but don't you think you could put a nice scarf around your head? Or is this forbidden too? Many of my girlfriends here fold scarves and tie them around their heads, with a bow or without. Or a very broad band - surely those are not too expensive, don't you think?

I think this is the longest e-mail I've ever written. I am worn out and dead tired but I could go on and on.

It would be much easier if you were here in my room and we could have an endlessly long midnight talk - wouldn't that be fun? This has been the first time for ages that I even thought about fun!

I am so sorry I can't help you with that Jason - why don't you stop hiding and ask him directly about that accident? Couldn't he have changed since? If Lisa likes him that might be a sign he is different now. Sometimes those Rambos turn into quite likeable beings - if the movies are to be believed. Anyway, I'm only rambling.

I take a big kiss and wrap it into a heartful of very good wishes and send it to

you now! I hope that your problems will get
solved as mine have - well - nearly.
Good night, Ellie,
Love from
Freddie

@ @ @

Ellie's head ached with scrubbing. She had been under the
shower for what seemed like an eternity, shampooing her
hair as vigorously as she could, trying desperately to
reduce the glaring orange to a more muted shade of
auburn. The packet said that the colour would wash out
after ten shampoos, but it didn't seem much lighter to her.

Everyone at school had teased her unmercifully. Sarah
Button had said she looked like a burning matchstick and
when Mr Reynolds had turned the lights off to show the class
some coloured slides of Roman ruins, Hannah Carr had shot
up her hand. "Please, sir," she had said, "it's still too bright.
Ellie Finch's hair is glowing in the dark!"

And Mrs Braithwaite, who was the most sarcastic teacher
in the entire universe, had said that she hoped that the lack of
hair would make for easier access to Ellie's underused and
underactive brain. All in all, it had not been a good day.

But the worst was yet to come. In just half an hour she had
to be at the cinema, looking dead cool and being charming to

Jason Hill. Just thinking about it made her feel sick. If Jason did recognise her, she knew just what he would think. It wasn't true, but his type weren't likely to worry about facts; he would just want revenge.

She was feeling sick just thinking about it. Perhaps she could ring Lisa and make some excuse not to go. But even if she did, she couldn't avoid Jason for ever; when Lisa was in love, she dragged her victim everywhere with her and it wouldn't be long before their paths crossed at a party or down at the local disco. She might as well get it over and done with.

She pulled on her trousers and shirt and then started on her face. When Jason saw her last, she reasoned, she was ten years old, so if she put on loads of make-up and her huge, swirly earrings, she could get away with it. She knew she could. She had to. Her life depended on it.

She spotted them in the foyer of the cinema before they saw her. Jason was leaning against a pillar, sipping a can of cola and idly stroking Lisa's hair with his free hand. She was gazing up into his face with a look of undisguised adoration.

If I hang about for another five minutes, thought Ellie, it will be time to go into the film and I won't have to stand chatting. Then, just as it ends, I can jump up and say that I have to . . .

"Hey, Ellie! Over here!" So much for brilliant schemes. Lisa had seen her and was waving frantically across the crowded foyer.

"This is my best mate, Ellie," said Lisa as Ellie reached them. "And this," she added proudly, turning to her friend, "is Jason. My boyfriend."

Ellie could tell that she was savouring the phrase.

"Hello." Ellie met Jason's eyes briefly and looked away.

Jason took a final swig of cola and threw his can into a nearby wastebin. "Hi!" he said, reaching out a hand. "Great to meet you – Lisa's told me heaps about you."

He smiled broadly while gripping Ellie's hand. He really was incredibly dishy. It was hardly surprising that Lisa had fallen for him. But then, of course, Ellie reminded herself, Lisa didn't know what he was really like.

She pulled her hand away. How could she stand there, letting the boy who'd crippled her little sister pretend to be Mr Nice Guy? "The film's about to start," she said abruptly. "Let's go."

"So?" whispered Lisa as the final credits rolled. "What do you think?"

Ellie leaned back in her seat and stretched. "Wicked," she said. "I loved the bit where he told her that he was going to marry that other girl and she said . . ."

"Not the film, dummy!" hissed Lisa, jerking her head. "Him. Jason. Is he gorgeous or is he gorgeous?"

"Mmmm," murmured Ellie non-committally. "Look, I'm going to have to go because . . ."

"OK, girls!" Jason stood up and ran his fingers through his hair. "Where next? How about a pizza?"

Lisa shook her head. "You could take us to the pub," she suggested, leaning her head on his shoulder.

"Get real," he replied laughingly. "You're fourteen, remember? And knowing you, it wouldn't be lemonade you would be ordering."

"So?" Lisa pouted. "Go on – please. I really fancy a vodka and tonic."

Jason stood up and shook his head. "Nope," he said, edging his way into the aisle. "No way."

Lisa tossed her head. "Of course," she said provocatively, "I could go off you if you're going to be so stuffy."

Stuffy? Jason Hill? Ellie couldn't believe her ears. Jason Hill – who used to skive off school and buy cigarettes at the corner shop; Jason Hill – who stole a motorbike and injured her sister and got sent to a Young Offenders Institute? Oh please!

She pushed her way past Ellie and Jason. The memories were flooding back and she knew she had to get away. Her luck had held out this far and she wasn't going to tempt providence by staying any longer. "I've got to go," she began. "Loads of homework and . . ."

"You can't go yet!" protested Lisa. "OK, so we won't go to the pub – but at least let's have a coffee. See, me and Jason need you for another alibi."

Ellie opened her mouth to speak but Lisa was in full flood. "We're going away for a weekend together," she announced smugly. "To Brighton."

Ellie's eyes widened. "But you can't! That is, I mean . . ."

Jason laughed. "Don't look so shocked!" he said. "Lisa's making it sound like a dirty weekend – and it's not. My gran lives down there – she's got a flat on the seafront and it's her birthday next week. My parents won't . . . can't go so I'm doing the dutiful grandson bit."

Ellie stared. Duty and Jason Hill didn't go together. If he'd done the dutiful thing four years ago . . .

She shook herself. "Well, count me out!" she said rather more acerbically than she had intended. "I'm not going to lie for you!"

"But you have to!" Lisa pleaded. "You know what my parents are like – they treat me like some little kid. And I've never been to Brighton . . . hey! That's where you used to live, isn't it?"

"You did?" Jason exclaimed. "Whereabouts?"

"It was ages ago," muttered Ellie, her heart pounding. "Look, I must dash . . ."

"She won't want to talk about it," interrupted Lisa knowledgeably. "Her little sister had a terrible accident there, and their family moved away and . . ."

"*Shut up!*" Ellie hadn't meant to shout but she had to to stop Lisa talking. "Look, OK, I'll cover for you. Satisfied? Now I must go."

"Thanks, Ellie." Lisa gave her a hug. As Ellie looked over Lisa's shoulder, her eyes met Jason's gaze. His face was white. The smile had vanished. His lips were pressed together in a tight, thin line.

And in that moment, Ellie knew that he knew.

To: Friederike Hofmann <ahofmann@uni-bremen.de>
From: Ellie Finch <elliefin@email.com>
Date: Wed, 6 Sept 2000 23:18:36
Subject: **Big trouble**

Dear Freddie,
I'm so scared! When I got home and found your

e-mail waiting I was so relieved because it gives me an excuse to write back and try to sort my head out before I go to sleep. Sleep! That's a joke. How can I sleep knowing that Jason Hill is out there planning his revenge?

It was going OK until Lisa let it slip that I used to live in Brighton and had moved away because my sister got hurt. His face changed instantly. You could almost see his mind working, see him remembering the accident and working out that despite his threats, I had told the police that he had been riding the motorbike that ran Becky down. BUT I DIDN'T!! I really truly didn't. I figured that if my stepdad could lie, then so could I.

You see, a woman walking her dog called an ambulance and Becky and me were both taken to hospital. Mum came along and phoned my stepdad at his office but they said he wasn't there. Mum was frantic - sick with worry about Becky and desperate to reach my stepdad. I can remember it - she kept saying, "Where can he be? Oh God, where can he be?"

That's when I said, "He was in the park." But as I said it, it was as if his face was there, looming over me on the trolley in the Accident and Emergency room. I could hear him saying that if I told, he would throw me out. I imagined myself wandering homeless - oh, I

know it sounds daft now but then it seemed so
real and I was so frightened. So when Mum
said, "Ellie, what did you say?" I didn't
answer – and the nurse said I was in shock and
not to take any notice.

And then, later, when the police came to the
house and started asking questions, I reckoned
that it was safer to say I couldn't remember
anything. That way, I didn't have to tell about
Jason or my stepdad and no one could come and
get me. My stepdad told my mum he'd been at his
first wife's grave that afternoon – dead clever
because no one would be able to prove it and
besides, they all felt sorry for him and patted
his hand and changed the subject. I hated him –
and them – for that. So much.

They caught Jason, of course. He had dumped
the motorbike (which, by the way, was stolen)
in the carpark at the railway station. I guess
he thought he'd got away with it but the
police found traces of the wool from Becky's
cardigan imbedded in the tyre tread. They put
out an appeal on the local radio and someone
said they'd seen a teenager pushing a bike into
the carpark. The video cameras had picked it up
and they got him. They showed me his picture
and asked if I recognised him. I said I
didn't. Does that make me a criminal too,
Freddie? I guess it does.

Anyway, shortly after that we moved up here to Nambridge and I thought I was safe. Jason was sent to a Young Offenders Institute for eighteen months – and besides, people don't come two hundred miles to find you, do they?

Only now he's here and I know he knows who I am. He seems different – I mean, he was friendly and chatty and even ticked Lisa off for suggesting we should go to the pub and drink under age. But I guess that's all a sham. I guess underneath he's still the evil guy he was then. I don't know what to do.

Sorry – I've been going on and on about me and haven't said a word about you. First of all, HOORAY! I'm so glad your period came – it would be bad enough getting pregnant without having a two-timing sod like Marc for the father.

I couldn't believe that your father would actually sell your horse to meet his debts. But then I guess none of us really knows what our parents are like – I would never have thought my stepdad would go behind Mum's back and have an affair. Sometimes I think that when he goes off for days on end now, it's because he's found someone else. Mum says it's because he can't cope with what happened to Becky (by which she means he hates being under the same roof as me) but I'm not so sure.

Ellie yawned and glanced at the clock on her bedside table. Eleven forty-five. No wonder she was tired. But she had to finish this, she had to find out . . .

Ping! Her computer bleeped at her. New Message! At this time of night? She grabbed the mouse and clicked on the Inbox.

Marc. Two-timing, manipulating Marc.

Taking a deep breath, she read the message.

Dearest Ellie,
It is with good news this time I write! I have now saved the money for a small trip around Europe for the improving of my languages. And it is to England that I am coming first and so, dear Ellie, I write to ask may I stay a few nights in your home? It will be such joy to hold you again and to see your dear face. I know you too will be so happy to be with me. Write soon to say to me what day I am to come. Your Marc

Suddenly Ellie felt weary, dejected, deflated. Two weeks ago she would have been over the moon to receive such a message; now she felt used and diminished. How dare he? Or was she judging him unfairly? Was he really in love with her and just writing to Freddie to keep her happy?

It was no good. She was too tired to think about it. She'd worry about Marc in the morning.

She yawned again, rubbed her eyes and continued her e-mail to Freddie.

I'm *so* tired so I shall have to stop and go to bed. As for your suggestion about talking to Jason - are you MAD? He's probably got a gang of mates who would make life hell for me - and no, Freddie, he won't have changed. Those types don't. Must sleep, will write more tomorrow. Love Ellie

PS Just had another e-mail from Marc - you won't believe what he said! Tell you in the morning. Night night. *Gute Nacht, schlafen Sie gut!* Does that make sense? By the way, here is my German homework - could you do it again?

@ @ @

Rieke waved her arms enthusiastically in the air.

"And then I had my big scene!" she announced. *"The quality of mercy is not strained. It droppeth as the gentle rain from heaven upon the place beneath. It is twice blessed: it blesseth him that gives and him that takes. 'Tis mightiest in the mightiest! It becomes the enthroned monarch better than his crown."* And with this, Rieke reached out theatrically with one hand to heaven, while at the same time rolling her eyes until she looked completely cross-eyed.

The girls around her laughed and applauded. They stood in

a corner of the school yard as Rieke gave a demonstration of her Shakespearian experience in the summer camp. Her long blonde ponytail was swinging around her head as she changed position and continued: ". . . *the attributes to awe and majesty*," and gave a caricature of what she believed a truly majestic sweep with her hand, accompanied by fluttering eyelids, "*wherein does sit the dread and fear of kings*." With that she lifted her imagined crown like a hat and bowed in front of her shrieking audience.

"Welcome to the living," Anna whispered when Rieke had finished. "Seems you have finally arrived back home."

Rieke grinned. "Nice to meet you too." She could have embraced the whole world.

When Rieke got home she had terrible problems getting through on her e-mail, but eventually a message came from Marc. Even while telling herself not to expect anything nice from that cheating louse, her heart beat faster, as her eyes darted over the text.

Ma petite sorcière,
J'ai des nouvelles extraordinaires! Tu sais que
j'ai gagné des sous dans les dernières deux
semaines et maintenant j'en ai assez pour
acheter - un billet de train!

Rieke frowned. He had saved his wages earned as a waiter to buy a train ticket – so what? She read on:

Je suis toujours fou de toi et je veux te
revoir aussi vite que possible. Je compte les
minutes . . . Comme je suis un pauvre étudiant
je n'ai pas assez d'argent pour un hotel et
c'est pour ça que je voulais te demander si tu
peux trouver un coin chez toi pour dormir.

So he could not wait to see her again and counted the minutes, but as he could only pay for the ticket he was asking her to offer him their spare room . . . what a nerve!

Je t'embrasse mille fois.
Marc

Rieke sat there for some minutes and thought it over. Somehow she felt torn in two pieces: there was one part of her that longed for Marc, his caresses, his sweet and funny compliments – but the other part of her kept asking: and to whom else is he writing the same sentences? Even if he was completely exonerated as an honourable boyfriend, his two-timing was evident. Or was it?

She sighed and lifted Fritz from the bed. "You know something? I can't believe him any more. I just have to wait a bit and then I screw up all my courage and tell him what he can do with himself instead of coming here. I don't think I want to see him ever again – do you? No? Well, then, we make already two!"

"Are you sick or something? Since when do you talk to yourself?" Basti stood in the open doorway – she had not heard him coming.

Rieke blushed. "Fritz and I had a problem. But we've solved it." She hugged the black cat and put him back on the bed.

"Glad to hear it," her brother grinned. "It's bad enough with one member of the family needing therapy. Or is it in the genes?" He made a stricken face. "Could it be that I am two personalities? Dr Hoff and Dr Mann? And which one is now talking? Help!!!"

Rieke laughed. "Basti, you are the most ungifted impersonator the world ever saw!"

"Well, but I'm the world's best messenger-boy! Our mother, the lady of the house, is requesting our humble presence, since she seems to have something to tell us!"

"Oh. And when?"

"Now." He turned and she followed him down the staircase.

Inge Hofmann sat at the kitchen table drinking a mug of tea. She motioned them to sit down and didn't waste any time.

"Your father has arrived safely in Helsinki and is now looking for a train to take him up to the north. He seemed to be quite calm when I spoke to him, and I had the impression he is looking forward to one of his long walks, like the ones he used to make when he was a student and in the first years of our marriage. Well, let's hope he has a successful embracing of nature and comes back without any expensive urges." She took a long sip and smiled. "Actually, when I took him to the station yesterday evening he seemed already a little bit better. He has decided to grow a beard, because a razor weighs at least thirty grams and every extra gram has to be avoided."

She put her mug down. "The only bad news is that we'll

probably have to sell the house to meet all the debts he left. I'll still try to find a way, because I don't want us to lose our home . . ." Her voice trailed off.

"But . . ." Basti and Rieke looked at each other because they had said the same word. Rieke motioned him to continue.

"But I am only here every other day," he continued his sentence. "I'd be happy to move to Bremen – and you'd be much nearer the uni and Rieke would be right next to her school . . ."

". . . but too far away from Merlin," Rieke finished.

Basti shot her an exasperated look. "Oh, come on, grow up! Who needs a horse any more, when we can live in the city?"

"I do," Rieke said quietly.

"And I realise that," her mother assured her. "But if we have to move, Bremen is the most sensible choice. Well, I only wanted you to know how things are going."

Rieke mumbled something neutral and escaped to her room. She put on old jeans and short riding-boots, got her bike and pedalled as fast as she could to the Mertens' farm.

Just when she thought everything was falling into place – there came the next crisis! She leaned her bike against the stable wall, took the snaffle and went to the paddock to fetch Merlin.

There was a new horse standing right next to him – a nice chestnut mare. They stood swishing the flies off each other with their tails. But when she called Merlin he eventually came and she led him back to saddle him.

* * *

Later that night Rieke sat down again in front of her computer and looked eagerly for a message from Ellie.

Funny how much more important than Marc Ellie had become during the last two weeks . . . ah! there was something waiting for her. She leaned forward and started to read.

While digesting Ellie's last message very mixed emotions raged inside Rieke: anger, compassion, incredulity and fascination.

Then she started to write her reply:

To: Ellie Finch <elliefin@email.com>
From: Friederike Hofmann <ahofmann@uni-bremen.de>
Date: Thu, 7 Sept 2000 18:48:43
Subject: **Clueless but sympathetic**

Dear Ellie
Your story would make a good novel, but I guess
it's quite a different thing to live through one
than to read it. I wish I could send you a
ticket to come here. Here we only have an acute
shortage of money, a father on some survival
trip and some beastly brothers.

By the way: our precious Marc wants to visit
me. But why do I have the strange notion that
he doesn't really want to visit poor old me
but rather find a cheap place to sleep while
pouring out his rotten charm on every female
coming his way? Anna told me the other day

that he made a pass at her as well – seems he left no opportunity out. When I recall my deep-and-never-ending, oh-so-true feelings for him I feel like gagging! Maybe I should invite him to come and when he arrives you, Lisa, Anna and I and the rest of the camp should give him a nice heartfelt welcome! Sometimes, thinking of him makes me so furious that I could kick myself!

But how can you get rid of that Jason? Only what you wrote about him before he recognised you didn't sound that bad, did it? Perhaps he has changed after all? At least a little? Couldn't you talk about it with Lisa? She struck me as one of the most sensible girls of the camp – except for us, ha ha! Oh what a mess! And I'm sitting here feeling so helpless!

What about writing to your real father? Do you know the address? Do you want me to find it? Just give me the name! If only I had money to send to you to buy a plane ticket! Off and away!

Clueless, but with loads of love and sympathy,
Freddie

PS I'm doing your German homework now and will send it afterwards.
PPS My mother is threatening to move us to Bremen, which would mean that I couldn't see

Merlin as often as now. But today I met a girl named Birte, who has brought her horse to the same stable, and she lives in Bremen and already has her driving licence. She told me I could travel with her every time she goes to ride her horse, and she plans to ride it often.

PPPS Did I mention that she has a real hunk of a brother? Seventeen, tall, blond, blue eyes? But this doesn't make me waver in my resolve to stay solo for a while.

PPPPS How long is a while?

When next morning someone hammered against her door, Rieke thought she was still sleeping and only dreaming about noisy people disturbing her. But when she heard Basti's voice shouting, "Get up! Quick! Quicker! Merlin's gone!" she realised it had been no dream.

"Coming!" she cried and jumped into her clothes. Struggling with her sweatshirt, she stumbled down the staircase and rushed into the hall, where her mother stood in her bathrobe, talking into her phone.

"Yes, Mr Mertens, of course, we will come over immediately . . . No, I wouldn't call the police yet, we don't know for sure who has tried to steal him . . . Yes, yes, we are on our way!"

She pushed the off button and looked at Rieke. "Come to my room – I'll tell you everything while I put some clothes on."

But she didn't know much: only that very early that morning, Farmer Mertens had seen a big car with a horsebox near the paddock gate, and a bald man engaged in a struggle with a horse. When Farmer Mertens had rushed over to the paddock, he saw Merlin bolt and go thundering off, and the horsebox behind the car was still empty. The driver had been furiously claiming that he had paid for this horse and that he had returned to take it as it belonged rightfully to him. When Farmer Mertens had threatened to call the police, the man had climbed into the Volvo and driven away.

Dumbfounded, Rieke stood there thinking, This can't be happening – not again! Then they drove over to the farm.

Farmer Mertens was waiting for them in the yard and together they went to the gate. He showed them the tyre prints in the mud, and showed them a piece of paper where he'd tried to note a part of the car's registration number. Rieke's mother shrugged. "I am no Red Indian – I can't tell one tyre from another. Have you any idea where Merlin could have galloped to? Where could he have gone?"

Farmer Mertens shook his head.

"I have no idea. There is only one thing we can do. Rieke must take my mare Valeska and go and look for him. Vally is the boss of the herd and she will try to find him."

Twenty minutes later Rieke rode through the fields and into the woods, calling Merlin's name, but there was no response. Then, after what seemed an age, Vally whinnied for the first time and pricked up her ears.

She whinnied again and this time Rieke thought she heard an answer. Now Vally turned and Rieke gave her long reins and let her choose the best way to go. At the edge of a clearing, between three trees, they found Merlin, lying on his side, one leg stuck out awkwardly beneath some branches. Rieke slid from the saddle and rushed over to him.

"Oh, you silly creature, what have you done?" she sobbed.

Merlin's halter was entangled with a branch of a bush and when he'd tried to free himself he had obviously slipped and trapped himself in a lying position between the trees. How in the world was she supposed to move this huge beast?

Had he broken one of his legs? Would he have to be put down?

@ @ @

"So – um – did Jason enjoy the film?" What Ellie really wanted to ask Lisa as they ambled through the school gates the following morning was whether he'd said anything about her.

"How should I know?" retorted Lisa, brushing her hair over her shoulder and quickening her pace. "God, don't boys make you sick?"

Ellie raised her eyebrows. "I thought," she said, "that he was the love of your life."

Lisa's shoulders sagged. "He is," she admitted. "I adore him – he's so gentle and caring."

"Oh yeah?" Ellie couldn't keep the sarcasm out of her voice.

"Yes he is!" insisted Lisa. "Except last night he went all weird and silent on me – just after you left. For a moment, I even thought . . ."

"What?" Ellie spat the word out.

"Well, I thought he might fancy you," admitted Lisa. "Not that he would, of course . . ."

"Oh thanks," retorted Ellie. "Anyway, what made you think that?"

"His eyes followed you all the way along the road and then he kept asking stuff about you. In the end . . ."

Ellie's brain went on red alert. "What stuff?"

Lisa shrugged. "Oh – where you lived, what your mum did for a living, did you have any sisters – that sort of thing."

"So what did you say?"

"I told him that he was out with me and he could jolly well shut up going on about you, or he could forget the weekend away," she said. "You will cover for me, won't you?"

"Mmm," murmured Ellie. "So – did you say I had a sister?"

"Can't remember."

Ellie grabbed her arm. "You must remember – think!"

Lisa gazed at her in astonishment. "Maybe I did – anyway, what's the big deal?"

Ellie sighed. "Nothing," she said. "Anyway, what did he do then?"

"Said he was tired and went off home," retorted Lisa. "Didn't even stop for a snog in the bus shelter."

Her face clouded. "You don't – I mean – he didn't chat you up or anything, did he? While I was in the loo or getting popcorn?"

"Oh please!" Ellie looked at her in amazement. "If he'd even tried, I'd have had him."

Lisa's shoulders visibly dropped with relief. "I guess – after all you've got Marc, haven't you?"

145

Ellie's lips tightened in a grimace. "And that," she said, "is another story."

"So will you let him come and stay?"

Lisa eyed Ellie closely as they hung their jackets over their chairs and unloaded their schoolbags.

Ellie bit her lip. "I keep vowing to send him an e-mail telling him to get lost – and then I think, what if he really does adore me? What if this business of writing to Freddie is just his way of being kind?"

"It's not," interjected Lisa. "Take my word for it – it's not."

"And how would you know?" Ellie's nerves were frazzled enough without having her friend assuming that the chances of her being loved and adored were zilch.

"Because," said Lisa, scrabbling in the front pocket of her schoolbag, "of that!"

She shoved a photograph into Ellie's hand. "That's the one I wouldn't let you see round at your house," she added. "I thought it would upset you."

Ellie stared at the picture. It was Marc. And Lisa. And Marc's arm was round Lisa's shoulder. And worse, his lips were on her cheek.

"You cow!" Ellie exploded. "You – and him! You two got it together behind my back and . . ."

"Hang on!" Lisa interrupted. "Stop jumping to conclusions!"

She snatched the photo out of Ellie's hand and tore it into pieces. "That," she said, "is how much I care for Marc Fouquet!"

She tossed the fragments into the air. "He was like that

with everyone, Ellie," she reasoned. "You, that Friederike girl, me, Rieke's friend, Dominique in the kitchens . . ."

"What?" Ellie's eyes widened. "You mean . . ."

"Marc was — is — a flirt. Give him an inch and he'll take a mile. I wanted a picture of him and me as a memento of the camp; it was his idea to do the kissing bit. I told him to get lost."

Ellie's eyes dropped. "What a total idiot I've been!" she mumbled. "I thought, I really thought . . ." Her voice trailed off.

"You thought he loved you?" suggested Lisa gently.

Ellie nodded. "That type," pronounced Lisa, "doesn't know what real love is. Now Jason . . ."

At the sound of his name, Ellie's stomach somersaulted. Had it not been for Mr Timms appearing to take registration, she would have plied Lisa with more questions.

As it was, all she could do was pray as fervently as she knew how that Jason would forget all about her.

Even as she addressed the Almighty, she knew it was a pretty futile request.

"Now look," said Lisa at the end of the afternoon, "about next weekend. I've told my mum that I'm staying round at your place, OK?"

"That's crazy!" protested Ellie. "What if she phones, or calls round or . . ."

"She won't — and anyway, I've got it sussed. If she phones, say I'm in the loo and I'll phone her back. Then you can phone me on Jason's mobile phone — I've got the number here." She thrust a piece of paper in Ellie's hand.

"You can give me her message, I'll phone her back and she won't be any the wiser!"

Ellie sighed. "OK, but you're taking a big risk," she remarked.

"So?" retorted Lisa, tossing her head. "Risks are what make life exciting."

"It bloody was him – I know it was!!"

Ellie stood stock-still in the hallway, listening to the raised voices from behind the closed kitchen door.

"But, Dave love, it can't have been . . ." Ellie strained to catch her mother's anxious words.

"It was, I tell you! Are you saying I'm a liar?"

Ellie stiffened, her heart pounding. Her stepfather's temper was unpredictable at the best of times, but when people argued with him . . .

"No, love, of course not. But Jason Hill, here? In Nambridge?"

Ellie gasped, and gripped the stair post for support.

"I saw him this morning," she heard her stepfather declare. "I'd know that face anywhere. And when I made enquiries, the bursar said his name was Jason Hill and . . ." He paused. "He's just moved up here from Brighton."

Ellie's mother gasped. "No!"

"Yes," retorted her husband. "And I'll tell you one thing. I'm glad he's come. Because I intend to have him."

"No, Dave – that's all in the past. He . . ."

"Oh is it?" Ellie's stepdad was shouting even louder now. "Well, it may be in the past for him – and for you! But it's not in the past for my Becky, is it?"

Ellie heard his fist come down hard on the kitchen table.

"She's my Becky too," murmured Ellie's mother. "But we have to move on . . ."

"Oh do we? Well, maybe when I've had my say to that Jason Hill, and given him what for, maybe then we can move on, as you put it."

Ellie had heard enough. She belted up the stairs two at a time and rushed into her bedroom. As she crossed the landing, she heard the front door open.

"Dave, where are you going?" Her mum sounded frantic.

"To the pub," he replied. "To get my head straight."

Some chance, thought Ellie, sinking down on the end of the bed and putting her head in her hands.

Now what? If her stepdad really did confront Jason, he would be sure to tell Lisa – and Lisa would tell him that Mr Grant was Ellie Finch's stepdad and . . .

She shook herself. She had to work something out. But what?

She found herself walking to her computer, logging on and clicking on Outlook Express. New Message!

It was Freddie.

. . . Your story would make a good novel . . .

You could say that again. And Freddie didn't even know this latest bit. While her fingers typed the e-mail address to reply, her eyes scanned the rest of the message.

. . . Marc wants to visit me . . . Anna told me . . . made a pass at her . . .

Ellie couldn't believe it. Right.

To: Friederike Hofmann <ahofmann@uni-bremen.de>
From: Ellie Finch <elliefin@email.com>
Date: Thu, 7 Sept 2000 6:50:16
Subject: **Slimeballs!**

Dear Freddie,
So Marc wants to visit you? Well, guess what –
he made the same suggestion to me. He said he's
doing a tour of Europe – well, that says it all,
doesn't it? He's been using us – and others –
as a way to get free accommodation. It's not us
he wants – it's just a cheap holiday! I admit,
I almost fell for it. He talked about "my dear
face" and said he thought I'd be happy to be
with him. Happy? I'd kill him!

Lisa showed me a photograph of him and her
together, and he was kissing her – and what's
more he not only snogged Anna but also that
spotty Dominique girl who did the cooking. And
probably loads of others! God, how I hate him!

We have to do something, Freddie. We can't
let him get away with it. You'll have to think
really hard, and I will too. What a slimeball!

But right now I need your help about
something even more important. My stepdad has
found out that Jason Hill is a student at the
college where he is caretaker. And he's been

sounding off about confronting him over what
happened to Becky. Maybe you are right - maybe
I should tell Lisa and get her to warn Jason
. . . but WHAT AM I SAYING? Anyone would think
I wanted to protect Jason, which I don't. But
Lisa's my best friend and she should know the
kind of guy she's going out with.

It's nice of you to say that you'd like to
send me a ticket to Bremen - and I thought you
hated me! But I'm not so sure that seeing my
real dad would be a good idea. He went off
when I was three and now he's got two other
kids and only writes to me at Christmas and on
my birthday. He sends me cheques - but then
writing a cheque is the easy bit, isn't it? He
doesn't know anything about the real me.
Frankly, if I was going to Germany, I would
rather come to see you.

But your note did start me thinking that . . .

Her typing was interrupted by the shrilling of the front
doorbell.

"Ellie! Be a love and get that! It'll be Isla come for her
cookery books!" her mother called. "Ask her in and tell her
I'm on the phone to Gran!"

Ellie sighed and thundered down the stairs and across the
hall.

She pulled open the door.

And gasped.

It wasn't Isla. It was Jason Hill.

For a moment, neither of them spoke. Ellie stared at Jason open-mouthed, her heart pounding in her ears; Jason stared back, unsmiling and hesitant.

Oh God, what do I do? thought Ellie.

She opened her mouth to call her mother and then shut it again.

"Hi." Jason had found his voice. "Look – I, well, I wanted a quick word."

"If it's about the weekend, it's fine – I'll cover for you – I've got the phone number. Now I've got to go because . . ."

She tried to shut the door but Jason put his hand in the way and even she didn't have the nerve to slam it on his fingers.

"No wait – please! It's important. See – I think I know you."

Ellie felt sick. "Know me? Course you know me – we met last night!" She tried desperately to sound laid-back and upbeat.

"No – before then. In Brighton."

"I – what – I don't know what you mean!" Her voice came out as a high-pitched squeak.

"I need to know!" Jason stressed each word urgently. "It was you, wasn't it? With that little kid? By the stream?"

Ellie was too scared to speak. If she admitted it, he'd think she'd grassed on him and then heaven knows what he would do.

She felt as if her feet were glued to the spot, her limbs powerless to move. She opened her mouth but no sound came out.

Slowly Jason nodded. "It was," he said. "I can tell by your face."

"I didn't tell anyone . . ." she stuttered and then stopped, her gaze shooting over Jason's shoulder to the street beyond.

Staggering slightly up the opposite side of the road, his cheeks flushed and hair awry, was her stepdad. He was with two of his drinking mates and they had clearly had quite a few pints of best bitter.

And suddenly there was something even more frightening than having Jason Hill on her doorstep.

"Go! Now!" she hissed at Jason. "That way!" She pointed up the road in the opposite direction.

"No, wait – I must talk to you . . ."

"Then do it some other time!" she urged. "I'll see you with Lisa – anything – but just go!"

"Why?"

"That," she stammered, pointing down the street, "is my stepdad. Becky's father."

Their eyes met.

Jason turned. And then stopped. "I can't," he said. "I can't run for ever. I have to talk to him. To you. All of you."

Ellie stared back at him. His eyes were glistening with unshed tears, and a red flush was creeping up his neck.

What was wrong with her? Why didn't she just let him hang on and talk to her stepdad and get what he deserved? Only suddenly she wasn't quite so sure that he deserved what she knew her stepfather, assisted by the effects of alcohol, might do.

"OK," she said. "We'll talk. But not now. He's drunk. For my sake – all of our sakes – go!"

Jason nodded. "All right," he said. "But I have to talk to you. Tomorrow?"

She hesitated. "Please," Jason urged. "I'll be at the café in Eglinton Park at four o'clock. And I'll wait till five. OK?"

"OK." She was astonished at her own whispered agreement.

Jason turned, cast a quick glance down the street and sped in the opposite direction.

Ellie shut the front door and leaned back, closing her eyes.

"Where's Isla gone? Ellie, are you all right?" Her mum appeared from in the doorway of the sitting-room.

"It wasn't Isla, it was – a mate from school," improvised Ellie. "Wanting a Maths book. Yes, I'm fine."

And with that she fled upstairs.

Back in her room, Ellie typed furiously, having clicked back into her e-mail to Freddie.

You will never in a million years guess what has just happened.

For the next five minutes she hit the keyboard frenetically, pouring out the events of the last half-hour.

What shall I do? Shall I go to the café or not? What if I tell him that it wasn't me that told the police and he doesn't believe me? Should I tell Lisa? Or wait to hear what Jason says?

I know this sounds odd, but somehow he didn't seem as bad as I'd imagined; at one point I thought he was going to cry. I'm glad I made him

154

go: when my dad got back he was in a foul mood and I know something awful would have happened.

Do you know what really hurts the most? The fact that my stepfather comes out of all this whiter than white. And yet it was only because I saw him half naked with that woman that I ran off with Becky in the first place. I was so dumb - I should have realised that he couldn't throw me out because Mum would never have let him. But I guess when you're ten things aren't as clear cut as that.

And even now, I'm scared.

Please write back LIKE NOW - so that I get the note before I go to school. I need your advice.

By the way, I guess Bremen wouldn't be so bad - personally, I like towns because there's always something to do. But then I'm not horsy like you - to be honest, horses scare me! That's another reason for you to think of me as a wet drip. But I hope you won't.

Do write soon - about Jason and about our revenge on Marc.

What lives we lead!

Love Ellie

PS It's funny but I feel better having told you all this stuff.

PPS That brother of your new friend sounds a bit

of all right! If you don't want him, maybe I
will come and visit and have a look for myself!!
PPPS As for Marc - he's yours! And you're
welcome!!!!

@ @ @

Rieke bent down to Merlin and talked to him soothingly while
desperately trying to disentangle horse, halter, twigs and
branches. Twigs scratched her, thorns pricked her and she
hurt her bare hands on nettles, but finally she had him pried
loose and was trying to get him up.

"Come on, Merlin, be a good boy! Hey-ho, up with you!"
said Rieke, trying to stay calm.

Merlin looked at her, his ears twitching at her pleadings, but
he seemed unable to move. Rieke tried to feel if something
was broken, but the tears streaming down her face made it
difficult for her to see, and her fingers were cold and stiff and
did not tell her much.

Again it was Vally who came to the rescue, as her whinnying
got Merlin to move. Awkwardly he tried to scramble to his legs.
Rieke tried to help by pushing under his back and talking
encouragingly.

With a desperate attempt the fallen horse arrived at a
sitting position, but it was terribly hard work to make him get
up further. Shivering and covered with sweat Merlin finally

stood, while Rieke patted him and told him what a hero he was.

Slowly, slowly she led him to the path. He was lame in the leg which had stuck out so conspicuously, but he didn't want to be left behind: he wanted to get home.

Rieke unfastened Vally from the tree where she'd left her and while leading her, she called Merlin, who followed one slow step after the other.

It was the hardest work Rieke had ever done. Half an hour later they were met by Farmer Mertens and Rieke's mother, who had come looking for them. It took them two hours to get Merlin back to the paddock, because after every two or three steps he paused: he was obviously suffering from a haematoma and probably from pulled tendons, too. That was the diagnosis of the vet back at the farm, who was otherwise quite optimistic that after some days of quiet everything would be all right again.

Rieke thanked him with all her heart, while wondering how they would ever be able to pay his bill.

She squatted beside her horse and talked to him.

"Good old boy, you were wonderful – so brave and tough. But," she sighed, "if you hadn't bolted, all this wouldn't have happened. Farmer Mertens would have rescued you from that terrible man, I'm sure."

When Merlin had drunk a lot of water and eaten half a pail of concentrated feed, she left him and went to the farmhouse, where her mother was waiting for her.

"What about that horse thief? What are we going to do?" she asked her, anxiously.

"We?" Her mother smiled. "Nothing. I gave his car number to the police and they'll get hold of him. There's no way that your father could give him your horse as a security against his debts! That guy will never get away with that, no fear!"

When they got home, Rieke went up to her room to get some of the sleep she'd missed.

But when she entered her room, she thought about Ellie and switched on the computer. There was enough time for sleeping later.

To: Ellie Finch <elliefin@email.com>
From: Friederike Hofmann <ahofmann@uni-bremen.de>
Date: Fri, 8 Sept 2000 11:37:11
Subject: **Toughie!**

Oh, Ellie,
I can't believe it! Forget that cheat Marc - I think we both deserve someone better, Madam! Let's give him a real polite but devastating declaration of unending contempt!

But face it anyway - Marc really is not so important right now compared with your immediate problems.

I really don't understand why you are so afraid of this Jason. OK, four years ago he seems to have been a real shit, but everything you have written about him now shows him quite a different person - don't you think so? Maybe my distance makes me a bad judge of that, but

I would try to talk to him. If you are still afraid, you could ask someone to go with you - not necessarily Lisa, but why not Becky?

She must be old enough by now to be interested in what he has to say, don't you think so?

I'm afraid I'm not cast for the role of a counsellor, because I'm too far away and I don't know enough of the whole thing, but I'm never good at hiding something - I like it better if things are discussed openly. That's why I think you should tell your mother also.

Think of her being cheated for over four years and think what it did to us in only four weeks!!!

I'm not very well informed, but I'm sure there must be a government agency in your town, too, which deals with children and young adults who have problems with their parents. They counsel, they help, they give children to foster parents (which is probably the last thing you'd ever want) and even support people financially. OK, there might be a lot of stuffy dreary persons among those social workers, but perhaps you could find someone in whom you could feel confidence. Maybe they know the best way to deal with your stepfather?

I'm sure I'd make a rotten agony aunt, but this is all I could think of. In the meantime I hope with all my heart that you find a way to get out of that dreadful mess.

As to mess, we had the next crisis with my horse, but he still lives and will hopefully be all right in a few days. That scoundrel who came the other day to take him away because he lent my father money and thought that Merlin belonged now to him came back again this morning to steal him.

But Merlin bolted and ran off; unfortunately his halter got caught in the trees and he fell very badly.

It took us hours to get him back to the stable and I'm absolutely knocked out and over.

Hope you get my mail before you go out and I'm dying to know what happened during that meeting with Jason.

Good morning, I'm going to sleep!

Love, Freddie

When Rieke went back to the farm that afternoon Merlin was still in a bad way. She sat beside him and talked to him and tried to interest him in some treats to get him to stand up again, but it didn't work.

When the vet came half an hour later, he frowned and clucked his tongue. "This will not do," he said finally. "We will have to get him up. The longer he stays lying down, the worse it will get. It is a vicious circle; because of his pains, he won't walk, and not walking will make him so stiff that walking will hurt even more and he will try even less. OK, folks, let's call for help and start."

Getting Merlin on his hooves again turned out to be very hard work. They forced him up finally with the help of a blanket pushed under his body. Farmer Mertens, the vet, his assistant and Mrs Mertens heaved and pushed until the horse finally stood on his legs. But he leaned very much to the left and would have fallen down if they had dropped the blanket. They urged Merlin out of the stable and the vet told Rieke to pull a rope around the hoof of his hurt leg: every time Merlin took a stumbling step forward, she tried to get his hoof in a better position.

Rieke's new friend Birte arrived with her brother and both helped out for over an hour. Just when they were about to give up, sweating and exhausted, Merlin finally regained his balance. Something in his leg must have eased and slowly, and evidently in much pain, he walked alone to the hay and started eating. The vet gave him another shot and some ointment and declared he would be fine.

Rieke was totally exhausted and, turning to get her bike, she smiled wearily at Birte's brother.

"You want a lift?" he asked.

"Thanks, but I've got my bike somewhere here," she replied, pushing a strand of hair back from her face.

"So what? I can put it in the boot. Seems to me you are in no condition to cycle."

"But where is Birte?"

"She came in her own car."

"So you wanted to ride today, too?"

He laughed. "No thanks – actually I don't like horses very much. I came back to look for you."

Rieke felt herself blushing. "You really hit the prime time," she tried to joke. "But anyway you helped a lot. Thanks. Without all of your heaving and pushing Merlin would still be lying helplessly on the ground."

"You're welcome," the tall boy grinned. "Only don't make me do that every day. Tomorrow I will be stiff and aching all over. But I'll come and see if everything is all right with the horse, if you don't mind."

"No, why should I mind? I'm glad if I've got company while playing horse nurse. There is my bike."

He put it in the boot of an old big car and she told him where to drive. When they arrived at her home, he grinned again.

"So this is where you live. Now I know."

Despite all her weariness and worries, Rieke laughed. "I would have told you. It's no big secret. But thanks for the lift."

They got out of the car and he fetched the bike from the trunk.

"Thanks," she said.

"That's the third time you've thanked me. Are you on automatic?" he laughed. "Perhaps you could do me a little favour."

"Yes?"

"I still don't know your name. Or is it really just Rieke?"

"No, it's Friederike. And I've got an English friend who calls me Freddie."

"Male or female?"

"Huh?"

"The friend."

"Oh!" Rieke laughed. "Her name is Ellie."

He sighed exaggeratedly. "Well, that's all right, then. Bye till tomorrow!"

He waved and got back into the car.

"Wait!" Rieke called.

He paused. "What's up?"

"What's your name?" she asked, feeling stupid.

"Oh, excuse me – I thought Birte had told you. It's Markus."

He waved and drove off while Rieke stood there, thunderstruck.

Impossible.

This could not be.

She'd never dare tell Ellie!

But Ellie was the only one who would understand the crazy joke! The weird doings of fate! Of course she would tell Ellie!

When she entered the house, her mother called, "Is that you, Rieke?"

"Yeah!"

She entered the kitchen where her mother was laying the table, washed her hands at the sink and slumped down on a chair.

"Tell me everything! I called Farmer Mertens an hour ago and he told me how desperately you all worked to get that beast up! You should have phoned me!"

"Well, there were enough people. But it was really hard work, Mammi – I'm not so sure that I want to be a vet after all!"

Her mother laughed. "Heaven help! How fortunate it doesn't have to be decided tonight!"

Just as she sat down the kitchen door opened and Basti came in. In his hands he held a small parcel; he was studying it with a frown.

"Is someone expecting a parcel from a guy named so-and-so-müller? His scribble is even worse than Felix's and I can't make it out."

His mother shook her head. "Rings no bell with me. Let me see. But it is addressed to your father! He will know the sender."

"But Paps is away – shall I open it?"

Mrs Hofmann thought for a moment. "Well, you know, mail is everybody's personal affair. But as he is away for another four weeks at least, we might as well look to see if it is something important."

Basti fetched a knife and opened the little parcel, which was thoroughly sealed with tape. Then he reached into it.

"Must be some slips of paper."

He looked in and gasped. "No, look!"

He pulled his hand back – it was full of bank notes!

Dumbfounded he whispered, looking at the money. "They are all thousand-mark bills!"

To: Friederike Hofmann <ahofmann@uni-bremen.de>
From: Ellie Finch <elliefin@email.com>
Date: Fri, 8 Sept 2000 15:54:17
Subject: **Are you mad?**

Dear Freddie,

I guess all this trauma has done something drastic to your brain cells! Are you mad? Take Becky with me to meet Jason – the guy who ran her over and injured her so badly that she has to use a wheelchair whenever she wants to go more than five hundred metres? Expect her to meet him, when she had nightmares for months after the accident? Get real!

No – I'm going to meet him on my own. Well – hardly on my own. He suggested the café in our local park, and it's always packed at teatime with little old ladies and mums with toddlers. Come to think of it – he can't have any plans to get nasty, can he? He couldn't have chosen a more public meeting place if he had tried.

And as for suggesting counselling – no way!! Get that, NO WAY! I had enough of nosey parkers asking questions after Becky's accident; and yes, I know that there are nice counsellors, but they have a way of ferreting out the truth and then they would tell my stepdad and . . . Well, I'll leave the rest to your imagination.

What you said about my mum really made me think. When my stepdad goes off in a huff (several times a year), do you think he's seeing other women? Should I say something? But then again, how can I? After all, it was four years ago and she does love him. Why, I can't imagine.

There is one thing I do agree with though – and that's your idea about dealing with that slimeball Marc! How about we write a really wicked e-mail, telling him what we think of him! We could even send copies to all the other girls who were at camp – just in case he's been trying it on with them too! I feel better just thinking about it – they say revenge is sweet!

OK, I must dash – I'll e-mail you tonight and let you know how I got on with Jason.
Love Ellie

PS Since Marc is YOURS, you can start the e-mail off – I'll add my bit after you.

"You came!" Jason didn't smile, but simply let out a sigh of relief. "Can I get you something to drink?"

"No thanks!" replied Ellie shortly. "Just say what you have to say and let me get out of here!"

Jason gestured to her to sit down on the chair opposite him. The café was crowded with people and she had to push past a large woman demolishing an outsize chocolate eclair, and a couple of kids slurping milk-shakes through bendy straws. She almost wished she had agreed to have a drink.

"Well?"

Jason took a deep breath. "You're Rebecca Grant's sister, aren't you? Elinor Finch?"

"Yes!"

For an instant, Jason closed his eyes, then, biting his lip, he opened them and stared straight at her. "I am so sorry," he said, his voice cracking slightly.

For a moment Ellie was speechless. Was this really Jason Hill, sitting opposite her and apologising? Where was the guy who had threatened to come and get her? No, he was just trying to soften her up, catch her unawares. Well, stuff that!

"Sorry?" gasped Ellie. "Is that it? Sorry?"

Jason took a swig from the half-drunk cup of coffee beside him. "I want to tell you what happened . . ."

"I know what happened, if you remember," spat Ellie. "I was there."

Jason shook his head. "No – all of it," he stammered. "Look – just listen for two minutes, please. Please."

Curiosity got the better of Ellie's resolve to make him suffer. "OK," she said.

Jason swallowed hard. "All that year," he began, "things had been really bad at home. My dad had found out that Mum had been having an affair and he was in pieces. I mean, dead cut up about it. Mum said she wanted a divorce and he just fell apart."

He paused, took a deep breath and carried on. "I was so angry with them! With Mum for being such a slag – and with Dad for being so totally wet and wimpish, bursting into tears

167

and pleading with her all the time. I wanted them to do something, something to make things right again. And I guess that when they wouldn't, I thought that maybe I could."

Ellie's face puckered in a frown and she sighed impatiently. "What? What has all this got to do with what you did to my sister?"

A shadow passed over Jason's face and he flinched slightly at her words. "I started dropping out of school, playing truant, nicking things from the corner shop – I think now, looking back, I wanted to get into deep trouble so that they'd have to stop all their stupid bickering and do something."

Slowly Ellie nodded.

"Anyway," he continued, encouraged by the slight softening in her manner, "the night before . . . before it happened, Mum had come in at about midnight. Dad had been sitting up waiting for her – I know that because I was in my room playing a computer game. I heard her say that she was leaving for good the following day and that there was nothing he could do about it."

He took another gulp of coffee. "I went ape – I mean, I flipped," he admitted. "I yelled and shouted at them both, called my mum all the names under the sun and told my dad he was so wet it was no wonder she wanted out! Then I just stormed off!"

"What?" Ellie gasped. "In the middle of the night?"

Jason nodded. "You don't understand," he said. "I was beyond doing anything rational or sensible. I felt – oh I don't know, so . . ."

"Helpless?"

He eyed her closely and nodded. "Yeah – helpless. That about sums it up," he agreed.

"And? Well, get on with it."

In her absorption in his story, Ellie had almost forgotten her hatred of the guy and that would never do.

"I wanted to be alone," he said, "and as far away from them as possible. I ran for ages, through the town centre and up towards the old cinema. That's where I saw it."

"What?"

"The motorbike," he said softly. "Just leaning against a wall – not locked. Nothing. I took it."

Ellie's eyes narrowed. "So that was where you got it," she said.

"I rode out of town – I'd learned to ride the things on my uncle's farm, trail biking with my cousin – and in the end I stopped by this field and dossed down for the night. I didn't sleep – just lay there thinking about Mum and Dad and stuff."

"But what . . . ?" Ellie's question was interrupted by a tall, stern-looking waitress who tapped her heavily on the shoulder and glared down at her.

"If you're not going to place an order, I must ask you to vacate that chair," she intoned.

"I'll have a chocolate milk-shake," Ellie interjected swiftly. "Sorry."

The waitress sniffed and stomped over to the counter.

"Sorry," Ellie said to Jason. "Go on."

"The next day," he said, "I rode the bike all round town looking up my mates. I guess half of me wanted to get caught, but I wasn't. I wish now I had been."

"Me too!" spat Ellie.

"A gang of us went down to the park," he continued. "Of course I went on ahead, showing off on the bike, revving up the gravel on the paths and doing spin turns and stuff. Then I accelerated for all I was worth and bombed out of sight to wind them all up. That's when I saw her."

"Becky? But you couldn't . . ."

"Not Becky – my mum," he said, fiddling with the corner of the floral tablecloth. "She was with this man."

Ellie felt as if someone had thrown a bucket of ice cold water over her head. She tried to speak but nothing happened.

"They were standing in this little copse of trees," he said. "And they were – she was – you know."

Ellie nodded imperceptibly. "I know," she whispered, so softly that her words were lost in the babble of conversation from surrounding tables.

"This man – he was kissing her, and running his hands up and down her back. I stopped the bike; I felt sick. I moved closer and then I heard him: he seemed agitated, trying to calm my mum, saying something about not getting worked up about some damned stupid kid . . . I went wild – calling me a kid and talking about me behind my back!"

"I don't think you were the kid he was talking about . . ." Ellie began but Jason was too psyched up to hear her.

"I ran back and jumped on the bike, revving the engine for all I was worth. I rode right up to them, driving round them in circles. I was shouting and screaming and they literally leaped out of their skins."

He bit down hard on his lip. "My mum shouted at me not to be such a bloody fool – and that did it! The whole thing was too much, and I just roared off down the path – I couldn't see where I was going, because I was crying too much and . . ."

"And that's when you hit Becky," concluded Ellie. But this time her voice was soft and measured.

Jason nodded slowly. "I couldn't believe it," he said, with a catch in his voice. "I looked at her lying there on the ground, and then at your face so white and terrified, and I panicked. I don't remember what I said . . ."

"You said," interrupted Ellie, "that if I told anyone, you'd come and get me."

Jason shook his head in disbelief. "But naturally you did tell and . . ."

"NO!" Even now Ellie was desperate that he should understand. "I didn't – I was too scared. I told the police I couldn't remember anything and they said it was all because of the shock. Anyway, after a few days they caught you themselves."

Jason breathed out. "And I went to the detention centre and it was hell," he added simply.

"So why didn't you tell them?"

Jason's eyes narrowed. "Tell them what?"

"Who the guy was – the one in the park with your mum? You could have explained that you were so angry that you didn't . . ." She stopped. What was she on? She was actually trying to justify what this jerk had done.

"Anyway, why didn't you tell them?"

Jason turned and appeared interested by a sparrow on the window ledge. "Dunno who he was."

Ellie leaned across the table. "It's OK," she said. "You don't have to pretend. I know too. That's why I was running so fast. That's why me and Becky were on the path in the first place."

Slowly Jason turned to face her. "You know?" He didn't sound convinced. "Know what?"

"Who your mum was with," she said as calmly as she could. "I know, Jason. It was my dad. I'd seen them too. That's why they were so agitated when you saw them."

"You knew? All the time?"

Ellie nodded.

For long moments neither of them spoke.

Then Jason leaned towards her. "He paid Mum a lot of money to keep quiet," he said. "Mum wanted out of the marriage and he gave her enough to rent a flat away from Brighton. On one condition."

"That his name was kept out of it?" suggested Ellie.

"And that she made sure I went to jail — well, Youth Detention Centre, anyway," he concluded. "She gave evidence in court that I was a right tearaway and said she couldn't control me, hard as she tried."

"Oh, Jason! And you had to stand in court and hear him going on about Becky's injuries and you couldn't even say what made you drive so maniacally in the first place?"

He shrugged. "There just seemed no point. It would only make it worse to say anything. And it would have destroyed my dad . . ." He paused. "It's OK," he said. "I've done OK. I kept my nose clean and took GCSEs at the centre, and now I'm at college doing Media Studies. I want to go into journalism."

"Lisa said," nodded Ellie.

Jason looked alarmed. "Look," he babbled, "I know Lisa's your best mate and all, but you won't tell her, will you? I mean – she knows I was in the centre but not that it was . . ."

"I won't tell," agreed Ellie. "On one condition."

"Not you too!" Jason eyed her quizzically.

"I won't be your alibi for that weekend away," pronounced Ellie. "I'm done with lies and cover-ups. Either you tell Lisa's mum what you're doing – and surely she won't mind you visiting your gran? – or else you find someone else to do your dirty work. Agreed?"

Jason grinned. "Agreed," he said. "Actually, I think Lisa's being a bit dramatic about all this. I think she quite likes a bit of drama."

"You don't say," giggled Ellie and found herself smiling at him.

"So . . ." Jason began.

"So," finished Ellie. "It's in the past. You paid the price. So did poor little Becky. Sadly the only people who didn't were the people who made our lives hell in the first place."

So there you have it, Freddie. Tomorrow I'm
going to tell my stepdad what I know, and I'm
going to do it in front of Mum. I guess that's
what you reckoned I should do all along, wasn't
it? Well, much as I hate to admit it, you were
right. I know Mum will be devastated and my
stepdad will probably deny it all and go totally
ballistic, but that's a risk I'll have to take.
It's been eating away at me for four years and
I'm not going to let it carry on.

Sooner or later, Dad would be bound to bump into Jason and if he knows that I know, maybe he will have more sense than to open up old wounds and do something stupid . . . or violent . . . I don't know. All I know is that I have to do what feels right for me. For once.

What's more, I'm going to tell Becky that Jason is not bad. He did a stupid thing, but he was hurting and upset, just like I was. After all, it could have been me who hurt someone, the state I was in.

This all sounds mega-brave, doesn't it? I just hope I have the courage to go through with it. I can't believe that it's all come up again - Jason Hill turning up here! Lisa's boyfriend! It's extraordinary - maybe it's fate? I just hope it works out. Come on, send me an e-mail full of encouraging messages! And at the same time you can let me have the opening paragraph of our Oh-So-Revengeful e-mail to France's Biggest Cheat! By the way, what is French for scum? Slimebag? Two-faced little toerag?

Waiting in eager anticipation!
Love Ellie

PS He's dead meat!

@ @ @

Absolute silence in the kitchen. All three Hofmanns were staring and gasping for air.

Basti was the first one to speak. "But what . . . ? I mean, how . . . ? This is just too much!" He laid the money on the table and sat down.

Inge Hofmann just stared, her eyes big as saucers.

It was Rieke who started laughing. She burst from splutters to seizures and laughed uncontrollably and helplessly, and her mother and brother joined in. It seemed as if the tension and the uncertainty and the stress of the last weeks had found an outlet through bubbling, screeching, mirthful laughter. The tears rolled down their cheeks and they laid their heads on their arms on the table. Whenever one of them tried to stop the fit of laughing, tried to escape that merciless grip of unrelenting fun, he or she just had to look at the other two and they started off again.

It was a long time before they finally recovered. Still giggling and weeping at the same time Rieke asked, "But how much is it?"

Basti pulled the rest of the banknotes out of the envelope and started counting. Five little heaps lay finally in front of him. "Fifty thousand," he said with awe.

The three of them looked at the money, thinking, Where has it come from?

Would it solve their most immediate financial problems? Would they be allowed to keep it?

"Well," Mrs Hofmann said briskly, "please give me that envelope again. Maybe we can find out where it came from."

But the only legible part was the name of Jens-Jakob Hofmann and the address. ". . . müller" remained all they could decipher from the sender.

"I have no idea what it means," Basti moaned.

"All right, pass me the phone, please," said his mother. She dialled the number of the mobile her husband had taken with him.

". . . please call again . . . this number is not available . . ." said a recorded female voice.

"Shit," Mrs Hofmann said feelingly. "But I'll try again. We'll just have to wait."

It was only the next morning, when they met for breakfast, that Inge knew all about the money.

"You won't believe it, but it belongs to us rightfully – it's neither black money nor laundered nor stolen – sorry, Basti – but it comes from a friend of your father. His name is Hassenmüller, Bert Hassenmüller. Your father and he met some months ago, when the trouble with the gambling really started, and believe it or not, there must have been a night when your father won lots of money whereas poor Hassenmüller lost and lost. Your father was so happy that he lent that man some thousand marks – he doesn't know the exact sum even, typical of the state he was in, I'd say – and gave him his card. Hassenmüller promised that if he had a winning streak he'd pay him back ten times what he owed him and this is exactly what must have happened. So we have now fifty thousand marks and this gives us a breather – we can stay living here, Rieke can keep Merlin and we can pay vets and debts and . . ." She looked at her two youngest children and they saw that she had tears in her eyes. Rieke jumped up from her place and hugged her mother. Basti came round and gave his "two women" a big kiss.

"You both are super, or mega, or however you call it nowadays," their mother continued, laughing, while wiping the tears from her eyes. "I think you bore all that trouble admirably – I wouldn't have known how to get through these last weeks without you – mind you," she shot Rieke a glance, "I could have done with a little less horse business, but that was not your fault either." She gave a deep sigh which seemed to come from the bottom of her heart. "Consider yourselves both the proud owners of a thousand marks. That is your interest for all the stress you had to go through." She laughed at their unbelieving faces. "I think I can manage with the rest. By the way, your father sends you his never-ending love – don't choke, he means it – and he wants some money to buy winter clothes as September in Finland is already quite cold, and he wants to stay there during October too. I think we can spare him some groschen to buy new mittens, don't you agree?"

After lunch Rieke went to the Mertens' farm, still afraid of what she would see. Merlin lying helplessly on the ground? Or Merlin cantering around like he did before?

As it turned out he was doing neither. But he was walking – still slowly and obviously painfully, but quite secure on his hooves.

She put his ointment where it was needed, gave him more hay and oats and saw to it that he had enough water. When she finally turned to go to the farmhouse, Markus was waiting behind the paddock fence.

"He seems much better today," Markus said when she came to him.

"Hmm." Rieke looked at him guardedly. Yesterday it had been so easy to communicate because her head and heart had been full of worries, but today it was different. He is at least three years older than me, she told herself. And I'm not keen on a repetition of that falling in love I made such a terrible business of at Lac Léon.

"I thought about what you said yesterday – why I don't ride Birte's horse? So I wanted to ask you if you'd give me some lessons – because you can never learn from a big sister, that's for sure." He grinned at her in his infectious manner and she found herself grinning back.

"Sure, why not? – if you can pay."

"Well, that's exactly the point," he admitted. "My money goes straight into that lovely old car. So my only chance would be if I could act as your chauffeur from time to time to pay you for the riding lessons." He looked at her expectantly.

"Well . . ." Rieke suddenly realised that she had not had a light-hearted, funny conversation in ages. "We could give it a try. You could start by giving me a lift now, how about that?"

* * *

When she got home, Rieke stomped up to her room, eager for news from Ellie.

She found an e-mail, but it was from Marc. Strange – she was truly disappointed that there was no message from Ellie! Only a short time ago it would have been quite the other way round! Impatiently she read:

. . . je suis désolé parce que tu ne m'as pas répondu. Comme j'ai dû trouvé une place pour quelques nuits en Pays-Bas et en Danemark je voudrais bien savoir si je pourrais faire un stop en Bremen pour te revoir et pour te chuchoter des jolies choses dans tes jolies oreilles. Écris-moi vite, ma chérie, ma petite sorcière blonde avec des yeux extraordinairement bleus . . .

So he still found her pretty, but obviously only because he needed a B&B on his travel through Europe. He had already found places in the Netherlands and Denmark? Well, hadn't there been that freckled girl from Utrecht, the one who played the piano in the concert group? And hadn't one member of the choir come from Bornholm? Had this Marc had love affairs with everybody in the camp? Unbelievable! That cheap liar, chatting girls up so that he could use them as providers of free hotels! NO WAY!

Immediately she started to tell Ellie all about it.

. . . can you imagine that louse? This is where

the shit hits the fan, as our English teacher
used to say to get us more interested in his
subject. What shall we do? I really want to
give him a good smacking farewell for ever . . .

Suddenly there was a sound to indicate another message had
come. Two from Ellie!

Breathlessly Rieke read Ellie's account of the meeting with
Jason, her eyes darting over the letters. At some words she
had to stop and think of the right translation and then she
hurried on. Goodness! Ellie asked for encouragement . . .
Rieke sat there, staring mesmerised at the screen, and finally
replied.

Dear Ellie
. . . just got your mail. I'll try to send you
all I can think of to help you through that
showdown with your stepfather:
  - a very special e-mail potion mixed with
strength, courage and determination;
- a cup of fervent wishes of your succeeding in
convincing your mother to stand up against that
cheating husband;
- a pill of conviction you're doing the right
thing;
- a box of giggles when things start to get too
serious;
- a truckload of the never-flinching, typical
Ellie Finch impudence!

- a pound of ardent desire to change that
terrible situation;
- a mega trolley of help from other people
concerned, and
- a basketful of my never-wavering belief that
things have to come out in the open to get a
grip on them. See what it has done for us!
(Only think of us having remained silent and
each of us snuggling in her belief she was
Marc's one and only girlfriend! And giving him
shelter just like ten other girls all around
Europe!)

I only hope you can use some of the stuff
I'm sending - but here comes the one gift
which will perhaps make the real difference: I
can send you the money for a ticket to
Germany, because I just got a THOUSAND MARKS! I
think that after having paid for Merlin's
medicine and the vet there will be enough to
buy you a ticket and off you go!

Think of this when things are starting to
get tough: whatever they do to you, whatever
they say - if it is too much to bear you come
here and we'll sort everything out.

I REALLY MEAN IT - THE MONEY IS YOURS
WHENEVER YOU SAY SO! This is all I can offer,
Ellie. But I'm with you and once you're in
your battle think of me wishing you pots of
luck that everything turns out much better than

you can think now! I sit here and keep my
fingers crossed (and toes and hooves and paws –
you remember Fritz?).

   I hope you come through all this as well as
possible: you deserve this!
Waiting for news!
Love and a big kiss
from Freddie

To: Ellie Finch <elliefin@email.com>
From: Friederike Hofmann <ahofmann@uni-bremen.de>
Date: Mon, 11 Sept 2000 16:10:41
Subject: **Worried**

Dear Ellie
Where are you? It's been two days and not a
word from you! I'm worried. What's happened? Is
everything OK with your stepdad?

   I thought I'd send the start of our e-mail
to Marc. I think we should put this:

Dear Marc,
How very interesting that you want to stay first
with Ellie Finch in England and then with me,
here in Germany! Oh yes – we know all about
your two-timing, conniving little schemes and we
both think you are a rat of the first order! It
will be SO interesting to discover what your
girls in Utrecht and Denmark think about being

used the same way, won't it? And believe us,
they will know. You may THINK you know
everything there is to know about women, but you
clearly didn't realise that WE STICK TOGETHER.
Especially when the opposition is a little
toerag like you!

So, Ellie, what do you think? Are you going to
add something? Please, please, please write back
soon. I'm so worried!
Love Freddie

To: Ellie Finch <elliefin@email.com>
From: Friederike Hofmann <ahofmann@uni-bremen.de>
Date: Tue, 12 Sept 2000 18:22:43
Subject: **Frantic**

Dear Ellie,
I'm really worried. I even tried telephoning you
last night but there was no reply and now I
keep imagining you sick in hospital, or your
stepdad having locked you up somewhere because
you yelled at him. Did you tell him? What's
happened? Please, please let me know you are OK;
I can't even celebrate Merlin trotting today
until I know you are in one piece.
Your friend Freddie

@ @ @

Ellie read her e-mails with increasing amazement. Freddie was really worried! Only a couple of weeks ago they had been sworn enemies and now Freddie was making international phonecalls to check out her safety! Neat.

She clicked on to Compose Message and paused, her fingers hovering over the keyboard. Where should she begin? After everything that had happened over the past couple of days, her brain felt scrambled and her emotions . . . well, never mind those for the moment.

To: Friederike Hofmann <ahofmann@uni-bremen.de>
From: Ellie Finch <elliefin@email.com>
Date: Tue, 12 Sept 2000 21:34:12
Subject: **You won't believe this!**

Dear Freddie,
I'm OK - and thanks for caring. That's really
nice. I was about to e-mail you the night
before last when all hell broke loose. OK, I'll
start at the beginning.

I got myself all psyched up to confront my
stepdad and of course, as luck would have it,
that was the very evening he was late home. I
was dead agitated - I dropped a glass and I
burst into tears when Mum shouted at me and

184

told me to stop daydreaming and concentrate on what I was doing! That did it - before I knew it, I yelled back that if my mind wasn't so full of her bloody husband, I might be able to think straight. And then it just poured out.

She went very pale but she didn't say a word. I felt like it wasn't sinking in - so I went on and on about the fact that Dad had been with this woman, and that it was Jason's mum and that Dad had bribed her to keep quiet - all of it, pouring out like a great torrent. Becky was out, having tea with one of her friends; if she had been there, maybe I wouldn't have said so much.

I don't know what came over me, but I told Mum that I guessed that every time my stepdad went off for days on end, he wasn't really trying to come to terms with Becky's accident. I said he was probably having it away with some other trashy woman.

That was when Mum cried. Not noisy crying - she just sat there, white as a sheet, her shoulders shaking and tears running down her cheeks. I felt awful. I went over and put my arm round her and she didn't shove me away.

And then she said something that made me understand why the books talk about your blood running cold. She just looked up at me and said "I know." Just like that.

It appears she's known for ages (or at least, had a pretty good idea) that my stepdad had affairs. And she's turned a blind eye because of me and Becky. She said that she couldn't have afforded to leave my stepdad and bring us up on her own, so she made the best of a bad job. She didn't know about Jason's mum though – or about Dad threatening me – and that really cut her up.

Anyway, I made her some tea and stuff and we ate supper. Well, actually, that's a lie: we pushed it round and round on the plate.

When Becky got home we tried to sound all jolly but it didn't really work. Mum kept looking at the clock and wondering where my stepdad had got to. Half of me wanted him to get back so I could let him have it – and half of me was dead scared of what might happen.

About nine o'clock the phone rang. It was my stepdad; he was ringing from the police station. Freddie, he had been arrested.

Ellie paused and rubbed her eyes, reliving the hours following the phonecall. Her mum dashing down to the police station, telling her to stay with Becky and not to leave the house for any reason whatever; the long wait, wondering what Dad had done – had he smashed into someone's car? Got drunk in the street?

Becky had burst into tears and asked whether Dad would

go to prison, and Ellie had almost said she hoped he would but stopped herself just in time. After all, he was a swine and a liar, but he wasn't a criminal and Becky loved him to bits.

Anyway, (she began typing again,) when Mum got back you could see that there was loads she wanted to say but she kept giving Becky sidelong glances and hesitating. She told her to go up to bed and then Becky just blew. I mean, BLEW! She said she might have legs that didn't work, but she had a brain, and she knew something was going on, and at ten years old she expected to be told the truth. She said she wasn't going anywhere until Mum told her what was happening.

You could see that Mum was totally gobsmacked by Becky's reaction and frankly, so was I. I mean, she's always been something of a goody-goody, sucking up to everyone, and suddenly there was this small fiend, slamming her fists on to the table and hurtling around on her two sticks shouting the odds.

At first Mum started a bit hesitantly. She said that Dad had been arrested for hitting someone and knocking them out. I knew at once. I mean, I just knew.

"Who did he hit?" Becky asked.

Mum was silent for what seemed like ages, but Becky kept pestering and in the end she said what I knew she was going to say.

"A boy called Jason Hill," she said.

Of course, Becky knew the name – she'd heard Dad shouting the odds about him often enough, and she asked loads of questions and Mum kept saying that Dad only hit Jason because he loved Becky and was angry about what had happened. Becky said you shouldn't hit people because it hurt a lot and sometimes it changed their lives. That made us all cry but I won't bore you with all the hugging and kissing bit that followed.

Anyway, Jason's in the local hospital with a fractured skull, but they say he'll be OK. Dad's due to appear in court next week and Mum's said he can't come home so he's in custody and it's all horrible. Lisa freaked when she heard about Jason and she is my best mate (well, alongside you) and I had to go round and tell her the whole story, which is why I wasn't able to e-mail you sooner. I thought she'd never speak to me again, but she was so cool about it; she could see that it wasn't my fault that my stepdad is a bully and a cheat. The one good thing that came out of all this is that Lisa's mum saw how devastated she was about Jason's accident, and quizzed me about it all, and I said that Jason seemed really OK now and had been dead honest and upfront with me. So maybe Lisa won't have to

go behind her mum's back every time she wants
to see him any more.

**Ellie stretched and yawned. She could feel her eyelids
drooping but she had to finish this. She owed Freddie that
much, considering how kind she had been.**

About the money - thank you so much! I think
it's brilliant of you to offer me a ticket and
yes, please, I'd love to come! But not now - I
reckon Mum and Becky need me around and besides,
dropping out of school would not be a good
idea. How about Easter? It would give us
something to look forward to through the winter
and would be dead good revision for my German
exams. Do you think Mum will divorce my stepdad?
If she does, what would that do to Becky? We
haven't told Becky about Dad and Jason's mum, of
course. Oh well, I can't worry about that now.
I'm too tired.

Your e-mail to Marc is ace. Here's my bit:

By the time you get this, at least a dozen
other girls from Lac Léon will have read it
too! So you will be known across Europe for
what you really are: a cheat, a womaniser, a
liar and worst of all, a scrounger.

No, we don't want to see you; no, we don't
need you in our lives.

Not yours in anyway whatsoever, Elinor Finch
and Friederike Hofmann

So there we are! Do you think we'll ever fall
in love again? Will anyone ever fancy me? Are
there any decent men on this planet? Oh well,
I'm off to bed.
Love, Ellie

PS I'm really glad we're friends. Here's to
Easter!
PPS Could you find me a dishy guy by the spring?

Ellie clicked the Send button and smiled. Freddie would write
back the next day, she just knew she would.
   She couldn't wait.

@ @ @

To: Ellie Finch <elliefin@email.com>
From: Friederike Hofmann <ahofmann@uni-bremen.de>
Date: Wed, 13 Sept 2000 07:59:15
Subject: **Looking forward**

Dear Ellie,
I am so happy it's out in the open now and you